CW00859448

THE CHATTERBOX SPY

JOHN MILLS YI

outskirts
press

The Chatterbox Spy
All Rights Reserved.
Copyright © 2019 John Mills Yi
v3.0

This is a work of fiction. Names, characters, businesses, places, events, locales, and incidents are either the products of the author's imagination or used in a fictitious manner. Any resemblance to actual persons, living or dead, or actual events is purely coincidental.

The opinions expressed in this manuscript are solely the opinions of the author and do not represent the opinions or thoughts of the publisher. The author has represented and warranted full ownership and/or legal right to publish all the materials in this book.

This book may not be reproduced, transmitted, or stored in whole or in part by any means, including graphic, electronic, or mechanical without the express written consent of the publisher except in the case of brief quotations embodied in critical articles and reviews.

Outskirts Press, Inc.
http://www.outskirtspress.com

ISBN: 978-1-9772-0932-0

Cover Photo © 2019 www.gettyimages.com.. All rights reserved - used with permission.

Outskirts Press and the "OP" logo are trademarks belonging to Outskirts Press, Inc.

PRINTED IN THE UNITED STATES OF AMERICA

Dedicated to my father Wai Kin Che, who taught me the way to wisdom and spiritual fulfillment

FOREWORD

The promise of a little known island in the Far East, Taiwan, continues to shine bright now with the election of President Tsai Ing-wen. As the country forges on under the shadow of mainland China, peace in the Taiwan Strait is now maintained through constant dialogue between leaders of the two countries. The young democracy of seventy years now stands as a testament of the wisdom and perseverance of the Taiwan people.

NOTE TO READER

All news articles in this book are purely fictional and should be viewed as such. Events and political figures portrayed, however, are accurate to the best of the author's knowledge.

CHAPTER 1

The curved ceiling of the Luce Chapel rose up on both sides of the church to the top to resemble a fishing net cast by Jesus Christ in the Sea of Galilee, an architectural gem designed in the twentieth century by the prominent Chinese American I. M. Pei as a home for those seeking shelter in a land where Buddha reigns. Beneath, Young Solomon Woo prayed and lifted his head up, his eyes captured by the criss-crossing patterns of the walls as his thoughts drifted away while the preacher delivered the sermon.

Woo stepped out of the Luce Chapel with a spiritual fulfillment which he always experienced at the end of service on Sundays, his faith founded upon years of education in a Christian elementary school run by an American missionary. Woo's faith in Christ was as solid as the stones which he liked to gather and play with outside his house.

It is a relatively young democracy in which Solomon Woo was raised in. An island that embodied thousands of years of history but which had been cut off from memory by fifty years of Japanese colonization. An island which endured international isolation but which developed over a short period of time to become one of the richest nations in the world.

R.O.C., short for the Republic of China, was sitting in a precarious position. U.S. President Jimmy Carter terminated relations with the island nation followed by the rest of the world in the year 1979. The threat of war with the communist rival across the Taiwan Strait loomed over Taiwan as speculation grew that the mainland will launch an attack. Lines of people began to appear outside the American Institute of Taipei seeking immigration to the United States.

Solomon Woo was headed against this tide. Born in Texas, he moved to Taiwan in 1979 with his father who accepted an offer to teach at Tunghai University in the city of Taichung.

The confines of the campus of Tunghai University served as a fun playground for young Solomon. The green, serene acres of the Christian institution gave Solomon plenty of space to explore with his bicycle. To the north of the campus boundary lies the Tunghai manors, a a loud, bustling neighborhood where students could find cheap rooms and apartments for rent. To the east stood the Veteran's Hospital Taichung, erected just a few years after Solomon arrived in Tunghai. To the south, the factories of the Taichung Industrial Park were busy spewing fumes which fortunately blew away from the campus by the downhill gusts of the Ta Du hill.

Life came in abundance within the walls of Tunghai University, situated on the central part of the tropical island. Behind Solomon's house, a bamboo forest divided his backyard from that of the neighbors. Toads were perhaps the most common amphibian sighted. When it rained, the reptiles could be found mercilessly squashed under the tires of the passing automobiles. Tunghai was also home for a diverse species of butterflies floating about the flower beds that lined the paved roads.

Every summer, Solomon's father would take him to visit his grandparents in Hong Kong. Solomon's grandmother stayed in a small flat in the affluent community of Happy Valley right across from the race track. "Ma Ma," was the salutation which Solomon abided by when he addressed his grandmother. She had a maid who stayed with her and took care of the cooking, laundry, and cleaning. Solomon only met his grandfather once, when he was only five years old. Both Solomon's father and grandfather were men of few words, and not a word was said to Solomon by his grandfather during their encounter in the summer of 1980.

Solomon's best friend in Tunghai, Huang, lived four doors down from his house in the faculty housing on campus. Huang attended the same missionary academy as Solomon and both of them took the bus to school every day together. Run by a southern Baptist preacher, Taichung Baptist Academy had a total student population of less than thirty, most whom were children of American expatriates. Solomon earned good grades and garnered his share of awards when it came time to the school's year-end banquet.

The prospect for war with the mainland was brewing, and war games were already being played out among the children who lived inside the protective walls of the Tunghai University campus. Solomon knew where to purchase his ammunition for the firecracker war which took place every Chinese New Year. Days before the national holiday, Solomon rode his bicycle across the road to a small grocery store where the owner kept an assortment of firecrackers.

Solomon bought water ducks, sky shooters, and b.b. rockets in quantities sufficient for the war of such magnitude. Huang had already built a rocket launcher out of pieces of wood and a plastic pipe. As darkness fell on the eve of Chinese New Year, Solomon and Huang set out for the elementary school. The two-story building was already being guarded by a dozen of heavily armed kids trying to suppress an assault by a larger opposing force on the ground. Solomon and Huang positioned themselves on top of a slide at the playground below the school building.

"This is a good spot," said Solomon. "We are high enough to get to them. "

"Put your head down. Someone at the second floor is lighting a sky shooter," said Huang.

Solomon and Huang ducked as the shooter whizzed past above their heads.

"That was close," said Solomon.

Huang drew out the rocket launcher and Solomon inserted a sky shooter into the plastic barrel. Huang pointed the rocket Launcher at a kid defending an outdoor terrace on the second floor, while Solomon lit the sky shooter And watched it fly right into the target area before the firecracker detonated with a loud bang. The helpless kid on the patio let out a scream to the satisfaction of Solomon and Huang. The constant crackling that filled the air was abruptly interrupted by the whistle of the campus police who descended upon the war zone. The kids quickly scattered and Solomon ran towards the bushes to hide. Such was the battle that would be repeated Every Chinese New Year and etched into the memory of the children who lived under the threat of war. Most of these kids will grow up to be drafted into the army as part of the R.O.C. government's policy of compulsory military service. Solomon, as an American citizen, would not be bound by that responsibility.

The fun, simple childhood which Solomon enjoyed was reinforced by his participation in the Tunghai Youth Fellowship. Solomon and his best friend faithfully attended the meetings every Saturday mentored by the counselor Kuo Ke, a university student at Tunghai whose mother ran the

Tunghai Elementary School as the headmaster. Pretty girls often attracted boys to the meetings and during then there would be dozens of them in attendance. The Tunghai Youth Fellowship summer camp was the highlight for Solomon. This particular year, the camp was being held at a facility by the beach about a two hour drive from the university. During sunset at low tide, the kids would capture tiny crabs which would crawl out from the sand.

At Christmas, members of the youth fellowship contributed their time to the Christmas play which would take place inside the Luce Chapel. Solomon took on the role of a Roman soldier who was bribed with a ruby for the release of an innocent woman. The sparkle of Solomon's eye when he ogled at the gem cast a spell over the audience.

Solomon could be classified as a wild tom boy if not for the discipline given by his father. Huang Shan Woo only needed to mention to his boy that he once fired a gun to earn Solomon's respect. For what reason and where Huang Shan fired the gun Huang Shan did not tell.

CHAPTER 2

It was a brisk summer morning in the year of 1987 when Sisy Liu answered the phone call That would change her life forever.

"Hello, who is this," said Liu.

"This is David Chang from the National Security Bureau. We need to talk to you."

"What is this regarding?"

"I will tell you the details when we meet. Please come to the Garden Hotel in Taipei tomorrow at ten a.m."

Since martial law was declared eight years ago, the R.O.C. government was been busily monitoring an underground movement for Taiwan independence. The disillusioned were mischievolously plotting for the day when they would gain power even when it meant building a beautiful lie to cheat the masses. The dream would remain just a dream to the end. The Tunghai University student was working secretly as a clerk who relayed messages between the leaders of the movement and perhaps the NSB had found out. The innocent Sisy Liu was pondering what she should do. Liu decided that it would be best if she followed the NSB's orders. She picked up the telephone and called her employer.

"I am being followed by the NSB," Liu said. "They want to talk to me in Taipei tomorrow."

"Be careful. I will inform the others." the man on the other end said.

The next day, Liu took the bus to the capital city, her mind going over any charges that the NSB could lay on her and the answers that will get her leaders out of trouble. The bus dropped Liu off two city blocks away from Garden Hotel and she set foot for her destination. She turned her head and made a 180 degree sweep with her eyes. A uniformed policeman stood in the middle of the street to direct the congested traffic that was typical of any major Asian city. Behind her, An elderly woman holding a tote bag was walking her dog and flashed a polite smile to Liu. Liu smiled back, turned around and released a light sigh of relief. Fifteen minutes later, in what must feel like ten light years to her, Liu reached the entrance of the hotel. Liu stepped inside the posh, five-star establishment and sat down at the lobby bar.

"One orange juice, please," she said to the bartender.

"Coming right up."

Liu glanced back and saw a middle-aged man in a blue dress shirt and black pants sitting on the sofa with a copy of the China Times newspaper. He put down the paper and approached Liu at the bar.

"I"m Chang from NSB."

"Nihao"

"We know you are a student at Tunghai University. We need you to complete an assignment for us. There is a professor at your school who we need to monitor. We need you to befriend him and place a tap on his home phone. In return for the completion of the assignment, we will pay you one million Taiwan dollars, enough for you to pay for your tuition."

"What is the professor's name?"

"Huang Shan Woo"

ONE MONTH LATER,

The East wind was blowing particularly strong this day, sending rain clouds from the Central Mountain Range over the Tunghai University campus as Sisy Liu carried her textbooks and registration form to the administrative office. She had penciled in her choice to change her major from economics to sociology and already selected her courses, one of which was titled "Sociology and media: The impact of popular medium in the twentieth century. Instructor: Huang Shan Woo." Liu duly paid her registration fees for the fall quarter at the administration office and handed over her course selection forms which was immediately approved and filed in the Registrar's office.

Li had gained some experience for the covert operation from the underground movement which she had committed herself to since her adolescence. Her uncle was a lawyer who defended a movement leader during the Kaohsiung Incident for organizing a rally during World Human Rights Day merely ten years ago and had acquired recognition as an hero among the dreamers. The pleadings for the Kaohsiung Incident Case was typed out by Liu in the basement of a seedy hostess bar. During the trial, Liu met Chen Shui-bian every week inside a room behind the bar to give him the documents which he would later use to free the activist.

NOVEMBER, 1970

Huang Shan Woo took aim at the target with his .38 pistol and released six rounds, all of which hit the mark, at the indoor firing range of the Royal Hong Kong police academy. The instructor examined the results and gave Huang Shan a passing grade, completing the final portion Of Huang Shan's six-month training.

A man of few words, Huang Shan chose not to tell anybody of his decision to join the force, including his mother. The day after his graduation ceremony, Huang Shan was summoned to the Captain's office, where he was assigned to go undercover for an sting operation targeting a human trafficking ring. The captain had reason to suspect that the criminals were tied to the Triads, the mafia that exerted wide influence in the Hong Kong underworld. The police received a tip that the human trafficking ring was hiding illegals in a small hotel at Wanchai for the past year, and the captain planned to place Huang Shan close to its activities as the hotel night watch.

THREE MONTHS LATER,

Huang Shan was reading the South China Morning Post behind the reception counter of the Magnolia Hotel when he first spotted the head of the human trafficking ring. The "Snakehead," as what the Chinese call them, wore a bamboo hat and carried a white sack over his shoulder. He entered followed by three people who must look like mainlanders. The man took a look at Huang Shan and expressed dismay.

"Where is Hon Chi," the man said.

"He left two months ago," Huang Shan answered. "Can I help you?"

The man hesitated, put down his sack, and signaled with his hand for the mainlanders to step outside before turning to Huang Shan.

"I need a room." he said.

"Sure. For how many nights," Huang Shan said.

"Seven nights. I do not want to be disturbed," the man said.

"I'll tell the cleaning maid," Huang Shan said. "Are you alone?"

"Yes, can I get the keys now."

"I would first need to see your I.D." Huang Shan said.

"I have stayed here very often before and they have not asked me for I.D."

"I understand. But I must follow hotel policy."

The man reached for his wallet and gave his Residency Card to Huang Shan.

"Bo Weibin, Age 46," the card read. Huang Shan recorded the information in a black book.

Huang Shan handed Bo the keys and took a glance at the mainlanders outside the door.

"You're in room 7," said Huang Shan.

Huang Shan waited until Bo stepped into his room before picking up the phone to call the his captain.

"Hello Captain Wei, this is Huang Shan. I might have found the snakehead. His name is Bo Weibin, Age 46, a Hong Kong resident,"

"I will run this through our records. I will call you back. Meanwhile, keep a close eye on him and write down the time when he leaves and when he comes back."

"He has reserved the room for seven nights," said Huang Shan.

"O.K. I will let you know if we find a match as soon as possible."

Thirty minutes later, the phone at the reception desk rang,

"Huang Shan, we found something on Bo Weibin. He has a prior conviction for drug trafficking while working for the mainland gang Tai Hun five years ago. Bo already has an outstanding warrant. This could be Our Guy. I will send the

Flying Tigers as your backup. Wait for my orders and report to me on any suspicious activities," said Captian Wei.

Huang Shan reached for his briefcase hidden underneath the counter and pulled out his .38 pistol and his radio. The three mainlanders outside the door walked in and Huang Shan watched them enter Room 7.

Thirty minutes past and Huang Shan was growing impatient for the elite force Flying Tigers that was scheduled to arrive as his backup. He picked up his radio.

"Calling flying tiger 001, this is Huang Shan."

There was no answer.

"Calling flying tiger 001, this is Huang Shan."

One minute later, there was still no answer.

Huang Shan decided that it was best to wait for his reinforcements outside the building. He walked out the door and took the elevator down to the first floor with the radio in his hand and the gun in his holster.

Ten minutes later, Bo Weibin emerged out of the building with his white sack in his right hand, walking right past Huang Shan on the sidewalk without noticing him.

Huang Shan could not wait any longer. He drew his gun and followed Bo.

"Stop, this is the Royal Hong Kong Police."

Bo began to run and Huang Shan aimed his gun at Bo's legs, waiting for a clear shot amid the pedestrians.

Huang Shan fired his weapon but the bullet missed Bo by half a foot. He decided not to give chase. Huang Shan watched as the snakehead disappeared Amongst the crowd and returned to the building entrance to wait for his backup.

The black Royal Hong Kong police van carrying the Flying Tiger team pulled up alongside the sidewalk, and the elite unit, armed with semiautomatic rifles and wearing full body armor approached Huang Shan.

"Huang Shan, what is the status of Bo and the illegals," said the team leader.

"Bo just escaped, but the mainland illegals are still at the hotel in Room 7."

"Show us the way, we will follow you," said the team leader.

Huang Shan and the Flying Tigers made their way up to the Magnolia Hotel and the team leader signaled for a halt outside the door of the room where the mainland illegals were hiding. one of the Team members kicked the door open, and the rest of the Flying Tigers stormed in with Huang Shan behind them. Inside the room, the elite unit and Huang Shan found the three mainland illegals tied to a chair with their mouths gagged.

One month after, with no trace of the snakehead Bo Weibin's whereabouts, the case was closed following the deportation of the three mainland illegals.

No disciplinary action was brought upon Huang Shan for his errant gunshot aside from a few words from Captain Wei and the quiet undercover policeman was then discharged from the force.

MAY, 1977

Huang Shan Woo stood and faced the American flag inside the Federal Building in Los Angeles before reciting the Pledge of Allegiance among a hundred other naturalized citizens in a solemn ceremony, marking a turning point in his life. It was a proud moment which Woo would remember after seven years of pursuing his doctor's degree at the University of Louisville and the University of Northern Texas.

The job hunt which followed the end of his scholastic career, as was typical of academics, was a process highlighted by anxiety and a sense of uneasiness. A three month search for a teaching position in the United States turned to no avail, and Huang Shan decided to take a job offer from Tunghai University in Taiwan as a professor.

In the summer of 1979, Huang Shan brought his four year old son Solomon to Hong Kong to visit grandmother. His anger at the injustices of the world continued even after his discharge from the Royal Hong Kong police force seven years ago and Woo hid higher ambitions.

The U.S. embassy in Hong Kong was a compound protected on all sides by tall metal fences that sat on a slope in Admiralty, a stone's throw away from the touristy Victoria Peak tram station.

Consul General John Hastings was reading the day's copy of the South China Morning Post when His phone rang.

"This is Hastings,"

"This is Debbie. There is a U.S. citizen named Huang Shan Woo who is requesting to see you," the secretary said.

"O.K. let him in to my office,"

Huang Shan Woo followed Debbie down a hallway inside the embassy proper to a door marked Consul General, John Hastings. The secretary opened the door. Inside a brush painting of a Chinese junk sailing on Victoria Harbor conspicuously adorned the wall. Huang Shan noticed a rare Ming vase placed on a wooden stand that had been given to Hastings by the governor of Hong Kong.

"Hello, can I help you?" Hastings said.

"My name is Huang Shan Woo. I have previous experience working as an undercover Officer for the Royal Hong Kong police force and I like to help you in any way I can.

"What is your profession now?" Hastings said.

"I am a college professor in Taiwan,"

"Here is my name card," said Woo.

"O.K. I will let you know if there are any jobs that matches your qualifications," Huang Shan left the office as Hastings read the name card from behind his desk. The Consul made a few scribbles and inserted the name card in a vanilla envelope marked "Local Contacts, U.S. embassy, Hong Kong."

JULY, 1989

The buzz of the fluorescent light hummed particularly loud this morning inside the CIA headquarters at Langley as the East Asian division analysts watched the TV news that was being broadcast from Beijing one month after the Tiananmen Square massacre.

Director Johnson has just received approval from the Senate appropriations committee which would help fund Operation Red Block to establish a permanent contact with the student leaders of the bloody protest, the lawyers who would represent them, as well as the General Secretary of the Communist Party Zhao Ziyang, who sided with the democracy activists towards the end of the movement.

Across the room, Analyst Todd Simmons was hunching over his desk as he sifted through a mountain of classified documents in search of the perfect candidate for the job. The op was deemed top priority, and Simmons had been searching for his spy for three days without sleep. The bell in his mind Sounded when he came over a vanilla envelope tagged "Local Contacts, U.S. embassy, Hong Kong" and pulled out a business card.

The card read "Huang Shan Woo, professor of Sociology, Tunghai University, Taiwan with the scribbles "Previous experience as undercover police at Royal Hong Kong police."

Simmons carried the envelope under his arm with a sense of excitement and marched towards Director

Johnson's office. He stepped inside and flashed a smile at Johnson.

"Any progress, Todd?" said Johnson, sitting behind his desk.

"There is a Hong Kong resident named Huang Shan Woo who is a former undercover cop For the Royal Hong Kong police. I think he is perfect for the op."

"Where is he now?"

"He is a professor at a university in Taiwan."

"I want you to book the next flight to Taipei. I will notify the American Institute in Taipei to arrange for assistance."

"Yes, sir."

THE NEXT DAY,

The China Airlines flight 005 carrying Simmons touched down at Chiang Kai-shek International Airport, named for the Generalissimo who once united China after the fall of the Qing dynasty.

Simmons was greeted at the arrivals hall by Steve Huang of the American Institute in Taipei, which is a product of the Taiwan Relations Act guaranteeing U.S. weapons sales for the defense of the island but which stopped short of a promise for military action if an invasion by Communists occurs.

"You must be Todd Simmons,"

"Hello,"

"The van is waiting outside, follow me."

A journalism graduate from Columbia University, Huang had opted to return to his homeland to work for the AIT information division to translate English press releases into Chinese for publication by the local media.

"You must get used to the hot and sticky weather here,

which many foreigners find unbearable, especially now in the summer," Huang said as he took the wheel of a black Mercedes.

"I have been assigned to West Africa before; Nigeria, Ivory Coast, Mali. It is not as bad here." said Simmons.

"So what is the political situation here now?" said Simmons.

"It had been quite tumultuous ever since the U.S. broke off relations with Taiwan ten years ago. The situation has eased now that the government here lifted martial law in 1987. The essentials of a democracy: free press, multiparty legislature, and right to congregate are now permitted. To be honest, I miss the good old days before this; life had been much simpler."

"Progress does come with a need to adapt," said Simmons.

Forty minutes later, Huang dropped off Simmons at the Ambassador Hotel in Taipei and made plans with him to drive to Tunghai University in Taichung the next day. Simmons checked in at the reception desk and received the keys to his suite. In his room, he finished his reading of the CIA country status report for Taiwan in his room and went to bed.

THE NEXT DAY,

Simmons woke up early and finished his breakfast in the hotel restaurant before sitting down at the lobby to wait for Huang to arrive. He picked up a copy of the local English newspaper The China Herald and began reading. The front page story was headlined: "Opposition party DPP announces candidates for year-end Legislative Elections."

At 7 a.m. sharp, Huang showed up at the hotel lobby

and led Simmons to the black Mercedes parked outside. Navigating through the congested Taipei City traffic took one hour and Huang Eventually reached the Sun Yat Sen Highway where the two cruised at the speed limit of 100 kilometers an hour heading for Taichung.

Two hours later, the black Mercedes carrying Simmons and Huang came upon Taichung proper. The city located in the central part of the island still had countless rice patties squeezed in between new residential developments. Huang and Simmons drove past the Taichung Industrial Park and quickly found their way to the entrance of Tunghai University, coined by locals as the most beautiful college campus in Taiwan.

Huang parked the van outside the main gate and walked into the campus with Simmons on their way to the administration office. A tree lined road led the two to a Tang Dynasty style building with a center courtyard and a plaque hanging overhead which read "University Administration."

Huang and Simmons opened the door to the Registrar's Office and saw a young man sitting behind a counter busy typing out course selection forms.

"We would like to have a copy of the faculty list," said Huang.

"Hold on, I'll get it for you.

The young man turned and opened a drawer from a cabinet, pulling out a sheet of paper.

"Here is the complete list of the faculty members and their contact information."

"Thank you," Huang said before stepping out of the office with Simmons.

Huang handed over the list to Simmons who scanned the list carefully. Under the Sociology Department heading, he found the name "Huang Shan Woo, 11-1 Scholar's Row."

Another name also stood out as the only foreigner on the list under the Philosophy Department: "Paul Lundquist, U.S. citizen, 24 Mei Nong Road."

Simmons decided to change his strategy for his approach to Huang Shan. Direct contact with him would attract too much attention. The safer way would be through an American who Simmons can trust.

Simmons and Huang walked down the hill towards the faculty residences, picking up their pace as they closed in on Lundquist's house which sat behind a wall of bamboo trees. He knocked on the door and a young boy answered.

"We need to speak to Mr. Paul Lundquist," Simmons said.

"Wait here, I'll go get him," the boy said.

Five minutes later, a tall Caucasian man with red hair came to the door.

"Who are you?" Ludquist said.

"My name is Todd Simmons with the CIA. This is Steve Huang from AIT. We need to speak to you regarding an important matter."

"Come in," said Lundquist.

The house was a rustic, wooden gem that was built thirty years ago when the University was founded. The wood floors creaked as Lundquist, Simmons, and Huang entered the Living room and sat down on the sofa. Simmons came straight to the point.

"Do you know professor Huang Shan Woo?"

"Yes," said Lundquist.

The CIA wants to recruit Huang Shan Woo for an operation that would take place in Hong Kong. We need you to bring him a message; tell him to meet me at the Twin Palms Hotel in downtown Taichung tomorrow. That's all you need to do."

"Sounds simple enough." said Lundquist.

"You are doing the country a great service," said Simmons.

Simmons and Huang took their leave as Lundquist sat, his mind curious as to the nature of the operation and why Huang Shan was chosen. Lundquist's job was simple yet the responsibility weighed heavily on him. There was no going back now; he would be better off if he did not know more.

THE NEXT DAY,

The bamboo grove adjacent to Huang Shan's house on Scholar's row rustled with the wind as Huang Shan prepared for his trip to downtown Taichung. The quiet man dressed himself in a white collared dress shirt and black pants before he checked in on his son Solomon who was still asleep in bed.

The training that Huang Shan received during his service at the Royal Hong Kong police came into use as he began his rendezvous with Simmons. Deviating from his daily route to the faculty lounge of the sociology department, Huang Shan headed north and took the narrow footpath through the forest to exit the campus from the east gate. He then boarded The city bus and twenty minutes later reached the Taichung Train Station, a colonial building Constructed by the Japanese during their fifty year occupation of the island. Huang Shan alighted the bus and made a quick survey before retracing his way back towards the hotel, which was located across the street from Taichung Park with its iconic twin pavilions. The professor arrived at the park half an hour before the scheduled meeting and took out a copy of The local Chinese language newspaper the China Times from his briefcase. The front page story was a report on the frenzied legislative elections in Taipei that the reporter described as typical of any young democracy transitioning from an authoritarian regime. Assured that there were no bogies tailing him, Huang Shan entered the Twin Palms Hotel and took the elevator to the room 217.

Simmons answered the door with a polite smile.

"Hello, professor Woo. Come in,"

The two sat down and Simmons started his pitch.

"The CIA will run an operation which will place an agent in Hong Kong to maintain contact with the student leaders of the Tiananmen Square Massacre and hopefully General Secretary Zhao Ziyang of the Chinese Communist Party. The mission is to bring them to the United States without the knowledge of the PRC government. This is a long term position and you stood out in our files as a qualified candidate with your undercover police experience. We have arranged for you to take on the cover as a professor at Lingnan College if you agree to the job.

"I will need some time to think this over," said Huang Shan.

"I will be in Taipei for a week at AIT. Here is my contact information," said Simmons.

"One week will be enough time for me to make a decision," said Huang Shan.

"I look forward to your call."

Huang Shan stepped out of the hotel and headed north with his mind focused on his surroundings. He noticed an orange Honda Civic parked along the curb with a middle aged man inside who was reading a newspaper. The man momentarily put down the paper and took a glance at Huang Shan as he walked past.

A bogey.

Huang Shan gathered his courage with a deep breath

and continued his deliberate pace. thirty minutes later, the professor turned the corner as he reached The Boulevard of the Three Civic Rights, named after the founding principles laid down in the ROC Constitution by the father of modern China, Sun Yat Sen.

The clamor of the city seemed to drown out any secrets in this young metropolis, its people collectively waiting in silence for any sign of hope for a certain future. There were no sign of bogies now.

The professor emerged onto the open road and flagged down a cab without turning his head.

"Tunghai University," the professor told the cab driver. Huang Shan adjusted his seating position in order to take a direct look at the rearview mirror. Convinced that the Civic which he walked past was not tailing him, Huang Shan sat back and mulled his options. his family was his first concern. Solomon would be a burden if he took his son along with Him to Hong Kong; he would have to be sent to the United States where he would stay with his Aunt in Los Angeles. The smoke was billowing out of the chimneys of the Taichung Industrial Park as its factories churned out pharmaceuticals and other chemicals ready to be exported to Hong Kong and China. As the cab whizzed past, Huang Shan knew that the job was his true calling.

Simmons waited for half an hour after Huang Shan left to begin his walk to the bus station where he will catch an intercity bus to Taipei. He grabbed his University of West Virginia baseball cap and stepped out of the hotel.

From the Taichung Park across the Twin Palms hotel, Chang Shan, who was sitting inside his orange Honda Civic, spotted the CIA analyst exit the establishment and recorded the time.

Huang Shan walked briskly from the Tunghai main gate

to his house excited with the new opportunity, ready to tell Solomon his plans. Solomon was watching the 8 p.m. soap operas when he saw his father enter the house. Huang Shan waved at him to come and sit with him at the dining table. This was how the quiet Huang Shan usually does to gain the attention of his son.

"Solomon, father will move to Hong Kong to take on a teaching job at a college there. you can either come with me to Hong Kong and attend international school or move to America and stay with your aunt. I suggest you go to the U.S. so you can prepare earlier for college."

"I will go to the U.S." Solomon said.

THE NEXT DAY,

Early in the morning at the end of Sunday service at the Luce Chapel, Huang Shan, a devout Christian, said his prayers and marched out of the church towards a new life which God gave him. He found the Public phone booth across from the church by the post office and dialed the number to AIT.

"Hello, this is AIT information division," Simmons answered.

"This is Huang Shan Woo, I accept your job offer,"

"That is great news. I need you to report to Lingnan College as soon as possible to fill your position as professor for the fall quarter. You will serve as our point of contact with the Tiananmen Square student leaders as well as Premier Zhao Ziyang. The CIA has been given clearance by the State Department to bring Premier Zhao to the United States if the plan plays out according to the book. The college will arrange for faculty housing for you on campus and you must remain there and wait for our instructions."

———

National Security Bureau deputy chief Chang Shan was sitting inside the briefing room at the NSB headquarters which was tucked alongside the hills of Yangmingshan in Taipei when agent Yao Cheng stepped in. In his arms, Yao carried AIT's phone records for the current month.

"So what do we have?" Chang asked Lo.

"There is a unusual phone call coming from Virginia, U.S. to the AIT which was made last night. Our source inside AIT, Yangtze 4, has informed me that Steve Huang of the information division had been assigned a task to receive an American who will be traveling to Taipei today. The identity of the American she does not know."

"I want a surveillance operation on Steve Huang right away," said Chang.

"Yes sir,"

THREE DAYS LATER,

Chang Shan pulled out his mobile phone from his brief-case while sitting inside his orange Honda Civic across the street from the Twin Palms hotel to call the NSB chief Wang I.

"Chief Wang, this is Chang. I followed AIT's Steve Huang and the American subject from the airport. They drove to Taichung yesterday and spent a night at the Twin Palms Hotel. Huang left the hotel this morning. Agent Lin is on him. The American subject just left the hotel ten minutes ago. What should I do?"

"Return to headquarters," said Wang.

———

ONE WEEK LATER,

NSB chief Wang I called a meeting inside the headquarters at Yangmingshan with a grave look as he glanced across the conference table in the meeting room.

"Our source inside the AIT Yangtze-4 has tipped us on a suspicious phone call made to the AIT information division by a Hong Kong national who is working as a professor in Tunghai Univeristy. His name is Huang Shan Woo.

"I want a phone tap at the house of this Huang Shan Woo. I want Chang Shan to plan and execute this operation," Wang said to Chang Shan.

"Yes, sir." said Chang.

————

"In a closed society, such as the one we have here in Taiwan or in China, the media carries a stronger influence on how people interact. I want the assignment on my desk before you leave. Class dismissed." Professor Woo said at the end of his sociology class.

Sisy Liu rose from her chair at the front of the classroom and approached Huang Shan.

"Hi, Professor Woo. My name is Sisy Liu. I would like to ask you a few questions on the upcoming examination. Can I come to your house?"

"Sure, I will be home at 4 p.m."

"I will see you then."

Liu gathered her textbooks and left the classroom, heading straight for the campus cafeteria where she will have lunch. The day before, Chang Shan had already prepped her for the operation.

Three hours passed and Liu picked up her backpack, walking out the door of the campus cafeteria and down the hill towards the faculty housing.

Professor Woo was already at the door when Liu arrived.

"Hi, Liu,"

"Hi, professor Woo,"

Woo and Liu stepped inside and sat down on the wooden sofa in the living room. She took a look around and spotted the telephone sitting on a coffee table.

"Can I get a cup of water?"

"O.K.,"

Woo left the living room to go to the kitchen.

Liu placed the bug under the telephone before hurrying out of the house.

CHAPTER 3

Solomon Woo first met Winnie Lam at the first general meeting of the Chinese Student Association during his freshman year at UCLA. She didn't make too much of an impression on him then, but it was during sociology class when Solomon began to know her better. An attractive girl with large brown eyes and curly black hair, Solomon recognized her as she was sitting in the front row of the lecture hall.

"Hi Winnie," said Solomon, as he sat down next to her.

"This class is supposed to be easy," said Solomon. "What major are you?"

"Biology," she said.

"Studying to be a doctor?"

"Yeah," said Winnie.

Winnie was a typical Chinese student who was trying to fulfill her parent's wishes of having their children grow up to become either doctors, lawyers, or engineers. Asians represent nearly forty percent of the UCLA undergraduate student population; most of them choosing economics, engineering, or biology as their majors due to their parent's influence.

The week before midterms Winnie and Solomon agreed to study together at Solomon's dorm. The night was still young when Solomon let Winnie pass dorm security before they found a comfortable couch at the lounge.

"I have some instant noodles in my room. We should have some if we want to stay up the whole night." said Solomon.

"No, thank you." said Lam.

"That is the only thing I know how to make, except spaghetti, which is my favorite food." said Solomon.

"I don't know how to cook either," Lam said. "Every time I go to the supermarket I go straight to the chips aisle. I don't do laundry either. My parents do it for me."

"You are a Dashiaojie," said Solomon, a Chinese term referring to the spoiled, oldest daughter of a big family.

"Why does everybody say that?" said Winnie.

The two talked through the night and Winnie left Solomon's dorm at daybreak. She left her phone number with him that night.

Solomon picked political science as his major with a concentration in international relations. His goal was to one day work for an international non-profit organization such as Amnesty International or in an international law firm. Bilingual in Chinese and English, he hopes to make his living his somewhere in Asia after graduation.

Two weeks after midterms, Solomon decided to take the next step and call Winnie.

Their first time out of the campus together was for Winnie's field assignment for her biology class at the L.A. Zoo. Winnie arrived at Sproul Hall in her sleek, new Nissan 300Z. with the sunroof open to an amazed Solomon.

The wind was blowing on Winnie's long, black hair as she and Solomom cruised on the 10 freeway under the southern California sunshine as they made their way towards the L.A. zoo in Griffith Park

"What do you like to do for fun?" asked Winnie.

"Lately, I've been going out with some of my friends to karaoke a lot."

"Call me next time you go; I want to go too."

A large number of karaoke parlors that offer Mandarin pop songs can be found in the ethnic enclaves of Monterey Park, Alhambra, and San Gabriel, a forty minute drive from the UCLA campus. Solomon, an avid Mandarin pop follower, had visited almost every one with his Chinese-speaking friends.

By the time Winnie and Solomon arrived at the zoo it was already noon. Solomon followed Winnie as she spent the afternoon moving among the enclosures and taking notes of the animals.

"What is your favorite animal?" she asked.

"The tiger," said Solomon. "I am born on the year of the tiger."

"I am the year of the ox," said Winnie.

She was one year older than Solomon.

Contrary to the stubbornness that is characteristic of an ox, Winnie was an easygoing girl who made many friends among both the ABCs, or the American Born Chinese and the FOBs, or the "Fresh Off the Border" Chinese who just recently immigrated to the U.S and spoke mostly Chinese.

At the end of their trip to the zoo, Solomon promised to call Winnie the next time he goes to karaoke.

The temptations of a college life did not escape Solomon. He picked up drinking in his freshman year, and every Friday night he and his friends would take to the liquor store just outside of campus to purchase beer using a fake I.D. that Solomon's roommate John Roebuck produced with his personal computer and printer. The fake I.D. was of inferior quality but the liquor store owner always turned a blind eye to it.

Solomon then carried the beer that he bought in his backpack to Lenny Kwan's dorm room where he, Kwan, and a group of other students drank while watching a Chinese movie on video.

———

A few days after the zoo outing, Solomon called Winnie at her apartment and invited her to karaoke. They met at the karaoke parlor 21st century in San Gabriel. Since it was Winnie's first time at karaoke, Solomon and Winnie decided to practice in a private room rather than singing onstage at the lounge in front of other guests.

Winnie could not read Chinese well and chose to sing a few English songs while Solomon picked from the list of Mandarin and Cantonese songs newly released in Taiwan and Hong Kong.

Karaoke was Solomon's comfort zone. Trained to sing in his school's choir by an American music teacher when he was studying at the missionary academy, Solomon sang the songs with ease and quickly made an impression on Winnie as a good singer. Early 90's Mandarin pop songs were characterized by ballads that often described the heartbreak and hardships of a relationship rather than the upbeat rock or dance songs of the western music scene. Although having never been in a relationship, Solomon was adept in developing his own interpretation of the ballads onstage.

———

Solomon had two roommates in his dormitory: Roebuck was Caucasian and Raymond Kim was Korean. By and large, the three got along well despite rarely going out together. Solomon went out with his Chinese friends most of the time after class, while Kim developed his own social circle after joining the Korean Student Association. The only time that the three roommates went out was when Solomon treated Roebuck and Kim to dinner at Olive Garden after receiving his first paycheck from a part-time job as a clerk at a warehouse where he helped logged the inventory.

Solomon sometimes felt sorry for Roebuck as he did not have his own set of friends, unlike Solomon and Kim. At the beginning of the school year, Roebuck took Solomon and Kim to a fraternity party along frat row right across campus. Roebuck did not pledge to join the fraternity however, and for most of the year, he kept to himself.

Early into fall quarter, Roebuck divulged to his roommates on the subject of his love interest. Solomon learned from him that he had an interest for Melissa Brown, who lived three doors down from their dorm room. His interest for Brown became widely known on the tightly-knit dorm floor where secrets hardly ever were kept. No one knew then, however, that an incident involving Roebuck later that year would rock the entire dorm floor.

On a night during spring quarter, Josh Mecham, a dorm resident, came into Solomon's dorm room and broke the shocking news. Someone had written a death threat on the mirror inside Brown's dorm room in lipstick. Also, scattered beneath the mirror were notepad papers written with the same death threat.

Mecham asked Solomon and Kim if they knew who did it. Both said they didn't know, but Britton became the likely suspect of the crime. To investigate the crime, Mecham waited until no one was in Roebuck, Solomon, and Kim's dorm room before going inside and ripping a piece of paper off a notepad which was lying on Roebuck's desk.

Mecham compared Roebuck's notepad paper with the paper which were scattered beneath Brown's mirror and discovered that the papers bore the same UCLA logo. Furthermore, Mecham determined from the edges of the papers that they all belonged to Roebuck's notepad.

Mecham reported his findings to the floor Resident Administrator who decided not to alert the police of the incident.

Despite the evidence, Roebuck claimed his innocence and denied any involvement in the death threats when the R.A. confronted him.

Roebuck came across Solomon as a nice person who sometimes made claims that were far-reaching. In the beginning of the fall quarter Roebuck invited Solomon to go streaking on campus. Solomon declined and Roebuck later boasted to his roommates that he had completed the act on the quad of the UCLA campus.

As the school year came to a close, Solomon and Kim agreed that they would look for an apartment together for the next year without Roebuck.

———

Every summer Solomon returned to Taiwan and this year was no different. One of Solomon's best friends from high school, David Yee, promised to meet him in Taipei. A son of a wealthy businessman in Taiwan, Yee was sent to the United States to avoid Taiwan's heavily competitive school environment that placed tremendous weight on the annual college entrance examination. Yee and his three sisters lived in a large, million dollar house that was purchased by their father in Los Angeles. A domestic helper was hired to cook their meals and clean the house.

———

Solomon had a neighborhood friend from Tunghai University who was working as a photographer in Taipei. Michael Wei owned a photography studio and his clients included members of Taiwan's entertainment industry, models, as well as ordinary citizens who paid to have their portraits done.

Solomon found Wei's phone number through his parents who were still living in Tunghai University and called to visit his studio one afternoon. Wei was working with a model when Solomon arrived.

"Hi, Solomon, sit down over there behind the curtains," said Wei.

The studio was about the size of a two-bedroom apartment and much work was done to convert the relatively small space into a fully-working professional studio that featured a graffiti-laiden wall face tagged to resemble the urban spaces of the U.S.

"I like your studio, Michael," Solomon said to Wei as he was snapping away at the female model.

"Thanks," said Wei.

"What is this shoot for?" said Solomon.

"This one is for a fashion magazine cover," said Wei.

Wei invited Solomon to a photo shoot of a Taiwan pop singer which was scheduled for the next day. The humble, gentle Wei took up photography while he was attending high school and living in his parent's house in Tunghai

University. He often passed by Solomon's house with his camera while taking photographs of the flowers growing alongside the road.

Taiwan pop singer Annie Yi showed up at the restaurant Hollywood Underground wearing a black cocktail address and a pearl necklace followed by her entourage and a few members of the Taipei paparazzi.

"Would you tell the photographer to hurry?" said Yi to her publicist. "I have to make brunch with Sally,"

"I will tell him right away," said the publicist.

Wei was cleaning his Pentax camera lens when Yi's publicist walked up towards him.

"Yi needs you to start now,"

"O.K."

The tabloids of Taipei of late have been following Yi's alleged love affair with Taiwan

music icon Harlem Tu and the few members of the paparazzi have received a tip that the two would meet here.

"Tell those dogs to leave," Yi said to her publicist.

Wei grabbed his camera and approached Yi with a polite smile.

"Let's get started," said Wei.

Solomon attained his first taste of a celebrity sighting as he stood behind the scenes of the photo shoot.

Before leaving the shoot, Solomon invited Wei to come to the United States and stay at his apartment through the winter break. The night of the photo shoot Solomon, Wei, and Wei's girlfriend went out to a club in Taipei where Solomon watched the two others dance the night away.

CHAPTER 4

For the start of her junior year, Winnie picked the psychology class Human Sexuality, and she asked Solomon, a sophomore, to join her. Solomon accepted the invitation and selected the class as one of his electives. He missed the class for the first two weeks, during which he borrowed notes from Winnie. He attended the class with Winnie afterwards and listened as the professor lectured on the survey results of the rate of HIV infections among sex workers in Thailand. Solomon found the class boring and rarely attended the lectures, performing poorly on the midterm and final.

Solomon and Kim found a two-bedroom apartment two miles from campus which they shared with two of Kim's Korean friends. Solomon made the daily ten-minute ride on his motorcycle to one of the free parking spaces on campus. Kim and his roommates, Jeff Cho, on the other hand, took the thirty-minute walk to school every day to save on parking fees.

On the weekends, when he did not ride home to the San Gabriel Valley to visit his aunt, Solomon participated in the Chinese Student Association activities; parties, dances, mahjong nights, or dumpling nights.

Solomon spent little time with his Korean roommates; Jeff Cho and Rich Song were born in the United States and spoke little Korean. Cho had just transferred to UCLA from a community college while Song attended art school.

One November evening, Michael Wei called Solomon from Taiwan and asked if he could come to Los Angeles with a friend of his and stay with Solomon at his apartment. Wei and his friend, who was also a photographer, were to come during the winter break for one week during which Solomon's roommates would move back to their parents' houses.

Solomon told Winnie about his photographer friends coming to Los Angeles and Winnie agreed to go out with them after they arrive.

Solomon picked up Wei and his friend Germaine at the Los Angeles Airport in his Camry and took them to Santa Monica where they had dinner. Wei and Germaine were savvy businessmen who wanted to make the most out of their trip to Los Angeles. Germaine worked as a wedding photographer in Taiwan and also owned a boutique shop in the upscale Taipei suburb of Tianmu, where a large population of foreign expatriates resides. After taking photographs of the scenery in Los Angeles for use in their catalogues, Wei and Germaine asked Solomon to take them shopping for props that they could use in their Taipei studio and boutique shop.

Solomon brought them to Melrose Ave. in L.A. where he thought that the trendy clothing stores would appeal to the photographers, which it did not, as they found the prices of the merchandise too high. The next day he drove Wei and Germaine to the Sunday flea market at the Rose Bowl where the photographers went on their treasure hunt.

After a full day of shopping, it took a major effort to load all of the photographers' trophies, which included a treasure chest, an antique phonogram, and jewelry into the trunk of Solomon's car, but in the end, the photographers left the flea market satisfied.

That night, Winnie and her roommate had a date with Solomon, Wei, and Germaine at an Asian night club in Century City, Los Angeles.

————

At the end of their one-week stay in Los Angeles, Solomon drove Wei and Germaine to the airport. After checking in at the airline counter, Wei and Germaine were told that the items in their luggage surpassed the weight limit allowed. Through Solomon's Chinese interpretation, the two photographers learned that they would have to pay the airline US$200 per person as a penalty for their overweight luggage. The two businessmen agreed to pay without hesitation, knowing that the profit that they would make upon selling the props in Taiwan would more than cover the amount of the penalty.

————

As Solomon and Winnie sat inside Solomon's car at a parking lot of a Chinese restaurant in Monterey Park, Los Angles, one late evening in December 1993, Winnie sounded a warning that was out of the ordinary.

The subject was the upcoming CSA ski trip which Solomon was planning on attending, and the fact that Winnie's archenemy Janet Kwok was going on the trip as well.

"If you and Janet are going to the ski trip, I might not be able to hang out with you anymore," said Winnie.

Winnie did not explain her reasons for not liking Kwok, but Solomon was not about to abandon his plans on attending CSA's annual ski trip to Lake Tahoe, having already paid the fees.

————

Four vans reserved under the names of CSA members set off for South Lake Tahoe one December morning. The CSA trip goers did not forget to equip themselves with CB radios to serve as communication between the four vans.

The CB radios proved to be an essential tool. As the caravan was traveling on Interstate 5 one van was pulled over by the California Highway Patrol for speeding. The incident was relayed by CB radio to all the other three vans which were behind on the highway.

The CHP officer did not issue a citation and the fourth van quickly caught up with the other vans which were waiting on the side of the freeway.

The CSA group, which included the CSA president, vice president, and treasurer, arrived at their cabin at South Lake Tahoe late evening. The area was covered in snow which fell just a day before, the group learned from the locals.

After leaving their luggage at the cabin, the group of twenty some UCLA students then headed to the local ski shop where they rented their skis and bindings. Solomon was put in charge of shuttling the group between the ski shop and the cabin.

The first evening at Lake Tahoe the CSA officers cooked hot pot, a Chinese dish which included vegetables, fish balls, meat balls, shredded beef, chicken, and thin noodles in a hot boiled in a large pot. The contents were then to be dipped with a mix of satay sauce and raw eggs before being consumed.

Full of energy, the group arrived at Heavenly ski resort the next morning to begin their ski adventure. It was the first time Solomon tried skiing, but he decided to forego the ski lessons and tag along with the more experienced group instead.

Solomon came down the bunny slopes with little problem, but his first challenge of the black diamond courses left him stranded alone on the steep slope. He quickly fell behind the experienced skiers and for the rest of the morning struggled on the intermediate to the advanced slopes.

Despite the difficulties, Solomon enjoyed the peacefulness of the gondola rides and the tranquil scenery of Lake Tahoe as it is surrounded by the snow-covered mountains of the Sierra Nevada.

By contrast, the more experienced CSA treasurer Greg Chang speeded ahead of the pack on his snowboard the entire day.

"Where are you, Greg?" CSA president Linda Lu called out on her CB radio as the CSA group assembled at the Observation Deck for lunch.

"I'm near the observation deck," Chang answered, before emerging from the top of the slope and gracefully slaloming down the black-diamond course in the amazement of the CSA members.

After eating curry rice cooked by the CSA officers that night, the young men of the CSA group discovered a Jacuzzi outside the cabin. About seven of them, including Solomon and Greg, changed into their swimming trunks and took a dip into the swirling hot water. Kwok was the only girl who joined them.

Solomon then realized that he and Greg were a part of the in-crowd in the school's Chinese student circles.

The CSA group enjoyed a buffet dinner at Harrah's Casino at South Lake Tahoe the third and final night of their trip followed by an excursion to Reno, where the well-heeled CSA members tested their skills at the black-jack tables and the others watched on.

On the last day of the trip, the CSA trip goers returned their ski equipment and set out for their drive home to Los Angeles. The group took turns telling jokes over the CB radio and eight hours later the group arrived back safely.

Before going their separate ways, the CSA group ate dinner at a café in San Gabriel Valley during Kwok invited everyone to her apartment the following week for a potstickers.

———

Solomon told Winnie of Kwok's invitation and told her that he would go. Winnie said that she will be going to a club the night of Kwok's party and would come to Kwok's apartment later to pick Solomon up.

Kwok prepared potstickers and alcohol for the party and around a dozen students came, including Greg Chang and Solomon. Solomon had more than a few drinks as the clock crept to midnight.

Dressed in a black top and black pants with her bra showing, Winnie arrived at Kwok's apartment knocked on the door. Kwok answered the door, and Solomon, who already had much to drink, stepped out of the apartment.

The dizzy Solomon put his arm over Winnie's shoulder and the two made their way to Winnie's BMW. Winnie drove Solomon to his apartment just ten minutes away and helped Solomon to the door as he fumbled for his keys.

Without letting go, the Solomon took hold of Winnie and pulled her down on top of him on the couch.

The two then moved to Solomon's bedroom and Solomon began to unbutton Winnie's top.

"No," said Winnie.

Solomon stopped his advances and sat up on his bed.

"I never had anyone do this to me before," Winnie said.

"Don't tell anyone what happened tonight," said Winnie, before leaving Solomon's apartment.

Solomon called Winnie a few days after and the two began talking again. Solomon kept his promise to Winnie and remained tightlipped on the incident except towards one person – Greg Chang.

Solomon and Winnie continued to go to karaoke together.

One moonlit night, Solomon drove Winnie to a turnoff on Angeles Crest Highway that overlooked the entire San Gabriel Valley basin. Winnie, on the passenger seat, leaned on Solomon and slept on his lap. Under the moonlight, Solomon looked at Winnie and kissed her lips.

The brief passionate moments did not last as Solomon later found a job in Taiwan where he would relocate. Friends had no clue as to what had happened to the popular pair.

CHAPTER 5

JUNE 2, 1989

Zhang Yen Ci rode his bicycle past Jianguomen Gate in Beijing at a steady pace, humming to the tune of the song Sweet Like Honey as he reminisced his younger years with his college sweetheart Zhang Yen on his way to work at the Ministry of State Security.

"Sweet Honey, your smile is like sweet honey." The words reverberated in his mind.

His father, a high-ranking member on the Central Military Commission, had given him a desk job at the MSS to fill his time after his son graduated from the prestigious Peking University.

Zhang entered the MSS building and showed his pass to the security guard, taking the steps to the third floor, which belonged to the secretive domestic intelligence division. His daily tasks as a file clerk was simple and mundane and the young man displayed little interest in reading the classified documents that he was placed in charge of passing out to the numerous analysts.

Half an hour before lunch break, Zhang's section chief Lao Yan telephoned him to come into his office.

"Chang Yen Ci, your father has asked me to tell you to bring a file back to your father's house. Here they are. Do not open them."

"Yes, sir."

"Go home now." said Lan.

Zhang picked up the vanilla envelope containing the documents and stepped out of the office. Zhang collected his bicycle from the bicycle rack and hurried on his way.

The young man joined the sea of cyclists on Jianguomenwai Dajie and headed east towards the fifteenth century Astronomical Observatory, the site where ancient Chinese scientists took to the stars to provide advice and guidance to the emperors on the fate of their kingdoms.

Despite the repressive communist regime, a glimmer of hope has entered the minds of the Chinese people with the introduction of market reforms by Deng Xiaoping. The notion for making a good living whether through owning a business or working at higher wages has been growing more noticeably in the coastal cities such as Shanghai in the east and Shenzhen in the south.

Zhang turned left at the observatory where he pedaled along Chaoyangmen Dajie for thirty minutes before arriving at a gray high rise apartment that stood out as the tallest in the Chaoyang District.

Zhang nodded to the security guard at the front gate and walked into the apartment complex. Taking the elevator to the eleventh floor, he grabbed his keys and opened the door to his father's apartment.

Shan Yen was sitting on his wooden chair facing the window when his son entered.

"Where is the file?" said Shan Yen.

"I have them."

"What are the documents?" asked Yen Ci.

"Something you should not know. Go inside my bedroom and put them inside the safe."

Yen Ci stepped into his father's bedroom and opened

the file. Inside were what appeared to be diagrams of rockets and rocket launchers that were labeled RT-2PM. From what Yen Ci learned as an aerospace engineer major in college, he could guess that they were long range rockets which China had not yet have the technology to develop. The writing on the diagrams was in Russian.

Yen Ci remembered the combination to his father's safe and placed the file inside.

As he came out into the living room, the telephone rang.

Yen Ci answered the phone. It was his college friend Maylee.

"Hello, Yen Ci. The guitar club at Beida is having a reunion at the Golden Melody Bar tonight in Wangfujing. The old bunch wanted me to call you to see if you want to come."

"I'll be there."

"See you there at eight."

Later in the evening, Yen Ci parked his bicycle outside the door of the Golden Melody Bar where he and Maylee performed in their college years. The crowd had been a mix of students and workers as it still was now. Inside, Zhang found Maylee and his old friends sitting behind a table holding their guitars.

"Hello, Zhang," said Maylee.

"Hi, Maylee,"

After greeting his friends, Zhang ran to the bar and purchased a round of Tsingtao Beers for the group.

"Zhang, there is a new bar in Sanlitun called The Cowboy that is looking for performers. You should check it out."

"Sure."

The old guitar club president Wen Xiaolo raised his glass for a toast.

"To old melodies and many more melodies to come," said Wen.

A moment passed as the group gulped down their beers to Unchained Melodies that the bar was playing in the background. A solemn Wei rose from his seat.

"By the way, the Beida student association is leading a demonstration at Tiananmen Square to commemorate Hu Yaobang tomorrow. Beijing Normal University is also going to be there. The BNU music club president Chai Ling told me that she is organizing students to be at the protests. From what I know, at least a few hundred people will be there."

"It's wrong that they purged him from the secretary general position before he died," said Zhang.

"I agree. But what would going to Tiananmen Square do to change the current situation?" said Maylee.

"We must show the government that we care about him and for the democratic values that he stood for," said Wen. "There is too much corruption going on now in government. The march is scheduled for the day after tomorrow. It will start from the front gate of Peking University, if anyone wants to go." said Wen.

"I will be there," said Maylee.

"Me too," said Zhang.

JUNE 4, 1989

At eight o'clock in the morning, Zhang Yen Ci quietly slipped into his father's room and gathered the rocket diagram file into a white bag while Shan Yen was eating breakfast in the dining room. Without saying a word to his father, Yen Ci rushed out the front door.

The government had already given the order to clear the demonstrators the night before and tanks and armored vehicles have been sent in to crush the protests. Zhang anticipated military presence at the site and brought his MSS pass. Zhang hopped on his bicycle and began his ride towards Tiananmen Square. Thirty minutes later, he encountered a military roadblock on Jianguomenwai Dajie where he showed his pass to one of the soldiers on guard.

"No one is allowed to enter," said the soldier.

"I work for the MSS. We have orders to collect information on the students."

"O.K." the soldier waved him in.

Zhang walked his bicycle along the sidewalk of the thoroughfare and heard a thunderous noise from behind him. A column of tanks was quickly approaching the roadblock and the soldiers on guard were preparing to clear the way. Zhang dropped his bicycle and walked towards the middle of the road carrying his white bag on his right hand.

The column quickly approached and Zhang walked towards the lead tank which abruptly stopped. The tank tried to go around but Zhang sidestepped in an attempt to block it from passing him.

The tank commander yelled from the vehicle.

"What are you trying to do?"

"I have important information in my hands relating to national security. I want you to turn back now."

Two police officers ran out from the sidewalk and grabbed Zhang, taking him away from the scene as the tanks rolled on amidst the chaos on Tiananmen Square. The two officers pushed Zhang in the police car and drove towards the Zhaoyang District police station. After arriving, He was brought past a frenzied group of police officers who were busy processing scores of protesters whom they arrested during the day at Tiananmen Square. Zhang was taken directly into the interrogation room.

"Let me see your I.D." the officer said after sitting Zhang down on the chair.

"Zhang Yen Ci," the officer read.

The officer noticed under the "Parents" column of the I.D. card the name Zhang Shan Yen.

"Zhang Shan Yen is your father?" said the officer.

"Yes," said Yen Ci.

The officer turned towards the other officer and discussed their options. He knew better than to draw the ire of a Central Military Commission member.

"You can go now," the officer said to Zhang.

A sober-looking Zhang pedaled on his way to his father's home with the white bag in the front of his bicycle. Along the way, the stereos in front of the storefronts on Dongzhimen blared out the latest news from Tiananmen Square. Government media reported at least hundreds were dead and thousands more were injured in what the radio news announcer said was a crackdown on an illegal civil protest.

Zhang reached his father's apartment and set the briefcase on the kitchen table as he saw his father watching the television from his sofa chair.

"Where did you go?" said Shan Yen.

"I went to Tiananmen Square today,"

"Give me back the file"

"They're on the kitchen table. I'm sorry father."

"I already reported the missing file to the MSS. You should go to your uncle's house in Hong Kong before the MSS captures you. You are my only son. I don't want to see anything happen to you."

Shan Yen walked into his bedroom and opened an envelope filled with a big stack of Renminbi bills. He took out ten thousand RMB and placed it inside a smaller envelope. Shan Yen walked back to the kitchen and handed it to Yen Ci.

"This should be enough to get you to Hong Kong. Go now."

JUNE 6, 1987 HONG KONG

The Air China flight landed on Kai Tak International Airport with a number eight rating. Landing at the strip beside the sea at Kai Tak was always tricky for any pilot. Yen Ci carried his small luggage and passed through customs with a relative visitation visa as was the case for any mainlander entering Hong Kong. He made his way out of the Arrivals Hall and hopped into a Dik Si: the red cabs which had run Hong Kong for decades before the modern MTR subway was built years later.

The cab dropped Yen Ci off along Nathan Road at Tsim Sha Tsui, the busiest shopping district in Hong Kong. The bright lights of Tsim Sha Tsui always fancied him since he was a boy. The beacon of democracy for China mainland, Hong Kong was and perhaps always will remain a heaven for mainlanders toiling their way inside a wall of oppression and repetition.

Yen Ci stopped in front of a clock shop and eyed the watches on display in the storefront window. A silver plated Seiko caught his eye. He stepped inside and asked the clerk to show him the watch. Yen Ci paid the cash and walked away with his first taste of western capitalism. Continuing on his way past the Peninsula Hotel, a five star establishment that faced Victoria Harbor, he decided that he wanted to splurge a little for his first meal in Hong Kong. Yen Ci walked inside and ordered a filet mignon at the French bistro.

Satisfied with the meal, Yen Ci short paced his way to the Star Ferry Terminal where he will make the crossing to Hong Kong island. Gray skies hovered over the Hong Kong skyline as the boat carried Zhang over to Central. Zhang hopped across the gangway and stepped towards the taxi stand outside the ferry terminal. The red Dik Si took Zhang through Admiralty and wound its way up Tai Peng Mountain where it stopped just short of Victoria Peak.

Zhang's uncle lived in a white, two-storey mansion that was enclosed on four sides by a black metal fence. He stepped up to the front gate and pressed the doorbell. Zhang's uncle, Zhang Shan Mou opened the door and grinned cheerfully.

"Yen Ci, come in!"

"Hi, Uncle Shan Mou,"

"Have you eaten yet?' said Shan Mou.

"Yes,"

"Your father phoned me yesterday and told me that you would come. Don't worry, you'll be safe here."

"I need to contact a professor here in Lingnan College. Father said that he could be able to help me escape to the United States."

"Who is this professor that you are talking about?" said Shan Mou.

"His name is Huang Shan Woo, a sociology professor. Father told me that he had met him at a symposium in Guangzhou six months ago and that he works for the U.S. government. Father gave me his name card."

Get some rest tonight. You can go see him tomorrow morning."

THE NEXT DAY,

The red Dik Si carrying Zhang sped through the cross-sea tunnel connecting Hong Kong island and Kowloon at a steady 85 kilometers an hour. After reaching the Kowloon side, it headed north and brought Zhang to the entrance of Lingnan College a half an hour later.

Zhang stepped into the campus grounds and checked the map, locating the Department of Sociology building. He crossed through the campus grounds and found the white concrete structure with the sign "School of Humanities, Department of Sociology" in front. Zhang checked the directory and found "Professor Huang Shan Woo, Office L102" listed at the bottom. He opened the door and walked through a narrow, fluorescent-lit hallway before stopping outside the door.

"Come in," a voice sounded out from inside.

Zhang entered the office and saw a middle aged man behind a large desk.

"I don't think we've met."

"Professor Woo, my name is Zhang Yen Ci. I participated at the Tiananmen Square protests a couple days ago and fled to Hong Kong. The PRC MSS is after me for stealing classified secrets. My dad told me that you can help me escape to the United States."

"What is your dad's name?"

"Zhang Shan Yen."

"Yes, I remember. A member of the Central Military Commission."

Huang Shan stood up from behind his desk and looked out the window. The fir tree was swaying against the wind as noon quickly approached. The professor wanted to help Yen Ci. He turned around and faced Zhang.

"Do you know any one of the student leaders at Tiananmen Square?"

"Yes, BNU's Chai Ling is a friend of mine."

"The U.S. government wants to help the student leaders at the protests. If you can bring Chai Ling to me, I can arrange political asylum for you in the United States."

"I will try to contact her," said Zhang.

"Here is my name card. Call me when there are any new developments. Be careful."

Zhang inserted the name card into his wallet and stepped out of the office. He exited the Sociology Building and quickly found a telephone booth about a half a block down the sidewalk outside the campus gate. Zhang took out his address book and found the number to his guitar club president Wen Xiaolu. He entered the telephone booth and dialed the number.

"Hello, Wen. This is Zhang Yen Ci."

"Hi, Zhang. Where are you?"

"I am in Hong Kong right now. Do you have the phone number to Chai Ling."

"What do you want it for?"

"I met a professor here who works for the U.S. government. He said that he can help the student leaders and Chai Ling escape the country. He said that if I can bring Chai Ling to Hong Kong he can also arrange political asylum for me in the United States."

"I heard Chai Ling has already fled Beijing. Here is the number to his parent's house."

"How are you doing, Wen?"

"After the protests, I dare not go outside my apartment. The police are everywhere looking for the ones at the protests. I talked to the bunch at the guitar club and they are experiencing the same situation also."

"I'll talk to you later, Wen."

"Be careful, Zhang."

Zhang hung up and stepped outside the phone booth. He took a quick look around him. It was noon and the students are hurrying on their way to lunch. The vendors on the sidewalk are busy hawking stationary items and souvenirs. Zhang walked down a half block and hailed a cab.

"Sha Tin," said Zhang.

The green Kowloon cab zipped past traffic with Zhang

sitting inside. For the first time, he was worried for his own life. Zhang knows that it was a matter of time before the MSS catches up to him. It was time now to visit an old family acquaintance.

Chong I Liang was a reputed tailor among the Hong Kong elite circle. He helped prepare the Ching Dynasty traditional men's dresses for many of the rich businessmen in Hong Kong, which was often worn during Chinese New Year celebrations. Shan Mou became good friends with I Liang after many years of patronage and even shared with him some of his private secrets. Yen Ci can still remember I Liang as a little boy during a Chinese New Year banquet at the famed Maxim's restaurant, wearing a black and gold long dress that had drawn the adoration of the ladies in the restaurant.

A half an hour later, the taxi driver dropped Zhang off in front of a traditional courtyard house surrounded by green, rice pattie fields. Zhang reached for the door ring on the front gate and knocked.

A twenty-something young woman with piggy tails and wearing a white flower-patterned Chinese dress appeared behind the door.

"Hello, who are you looking for?"

"Is Uncle Chong I Liang there?"

"Yes, who are you?"

"My name is Zhang Yen Ci. My dad and Uncle Chong are good friends. I am here to visit him."

"Come in, he is taking his afternoon nap now. Let me go get him."

Zhang and the woman entered the courtyard. The dragon-guilded ceiling that adorned the house stuck out to the sky, symbolizing wealth and power of the residents. Zhang and the woman came inside the house and were immediately met by an ancestor altar stand on the front hallway.

Three incense sticks were burning alongside a plate of food offerings on the stand which offered worship to Chong's dead grandfather whose named was carved on a wood plaque.

The woman disappeared into the bedroom of her father. Moments later, she reentered the living room with I Liang behind her.

"Zhang Yen Ci! What a nice surprise!" Chong exclaimed.

"Hi, Uncle I Liang."

"How is your father?"

"He is doing well,"

"How is his health?"

"He is in good spirits,"

"I imagine that he would be. He has been a military officer for as long as I've known him. All that training must have given him strength and a healthy body."

"This is Maylin, my daughter. Maylin, this is Zhang Yen Ci. His uncle and I have been friends for more than thirty years,"

"Hi, Zhang,"

"Nihao, Maylin,"

I Liang took a sip of tea that had been served to him from Maylin and continued.

"My daughter is studying at Chinese University. She is in her second year."

"What major are you?" asked Zhang.

"I am studying political science. It is important in these times for women to study in college. Did you study college?"

"Yes, I graduated from Beida."

"Did you go to the Tiananmen Square protests?"

"I was there,"

Chong I Liang sat back in his chair and waved for Maylin to come help him up from his chair.

"I must go back to my bedroom and rest. Do you want to stay for dinner?"

"No, Uncle Chong. I have to return to my uncle's house."

Zhang watched as Maylin helped her father walk into the bedroom. Maylin's long, black hair and slender figure caught Zhang's eye and he was immediately taken by the act of philiopiety: obedience and submission to their family elders as one of the most cherished values in Chinese culture.

Maylin walked back into the living room and sat in the chair facing Zhang, displaying a curious look at him.

"I am going to the stationary store down the road to get some paper art. Do you want to go with me?"

"Yes,"

The two stepped out of the house and began their stroll down the paved road along the rice pattie fields. The road led past a cluster of farms and a large green pasture where a small herd of cattle were grazing in the afternoon sun.

"Did you come to Hong Kong to escape from the PRC authorities after Tiananmen Square?"

"Yes, the government is going after everyone who is at the protests. Some of my friends dare not step out of their houses for fear of being captured,"

Maylin took one long look at Zhang and saw something different in him. His shoulders carried a weight that seemed much more than the common person and his eyes seemed to hide a past filled with secrets.

"Were you the one that stopped the tanks?"

"Yes,"

Despite the positive response, Maylin gave a look of a surprised person like one who just learned something that is probably much more than she should know.

"You are a brave man."

Zhang and Maylin came upon the stationary store and browsed through the shelves of Chinese stationary, including traditional paint brushes, black water ink, and paper. At the corner of the store, Maylin found her paper art: red paper cutouts that read Chinese characters of fortune and luck. She picked out one that read "Loyalty."

"I want to buy this one for you," said Maylin.

Maylin and Zhang approached the cashier where Maylin reached for her flower-pattered, cloth-woven purse.

Maylin stepped out of the store and handed the gift to Zhang.

"I want you to keep this and remember me whenever you see it,"

"Thank you," said Zhang.

Maylin reached out her hand and touched Zhang's, holding them while she looked into his dark, brown eyes.

"Will you come back and see me?"

"Yes, I will," said Zhang.

Zhang took the Kowloon City bus from Maylin's house and set foot on the commercial area of Nathan Road in Tsim Tsa Tsui. He spotted the Wing On department store where Zhang planned on making his phone call to Chai Ling.

"Hello, am I speaking to Chai Ling's parents?"

"Yes, I am Chai Ling's mother. Who is this?"

"I am a friend of Chai Ling. We met at a guitar club exchange back when we were in college. I would like to know where she is now."

"Chai Ling is in Yunnan, now."

"Can you give me her phone number there? There are some important matters that I need to ask her."

"Here is the number."

"Thank you," said Zhang.

CHAPTER 6

MSS director Chao Ming Hua walked into the conference room on the third floor among a group of thirty of his employees including the domestic intelligence section chief, the surveillance operation chief, and some of the communist party staff in attendance.

He stopped and gave a stern look at his hard-working staff.

"Comrades, there is an emergency situation. One of our own, Zhang Yen Ci, has escaped

Beijing after stealing classified secrets and bringing them to Tiananmen Square. The PSB has notified us that he is somewhere in Hong Kong. What is more alarming, we found out, is that he has been in contact with Chai Ling. Domestic Intelligence has informed me that she is hiding in Yunnan now. I am ordering surveillance operation Chief Chen Wen to organize a team of five to track down Chang Yen Ci in Hong Kong and kill him. Chen, I want your best men on the job."

"Yes, sir," said Chen.

"Meeting dismissed," said Chao.

The Hui tribe of a Yunnan Province village gathered at

the groom's house to celebrate the wedding of a Hui young man and a girl. The girl was only seventeen and worked as a tea picker at the tea fields. She met the groom, a truck driver, who carried the baskets of tea leaves on his pick up truck. Their parents agreed to arrange for their marriage, as was customary of the Hui tribe.

Hua Yang, a friend of Chai Ling, was invited to the wedding banquet. A twenty-meter long table was set up outside the house of the groom where the ceremony was held.

Chai Ling was invited to sit near the end of the table where she and some thirty of the villagers gathered over chicken, rice, and the local delicacies. Hua Yang sat with her and they drank wine until the wee hours of the night.

The next morning, Chai Ling answered the telephone at Hua Yang's house and heard the voice of a stranger.

"Hello, may I speak to Chai Ling,"

"Speaking,"

"This is Zhang Yen Ci. I have some important matters to talk to you about. I know you are hiding in Yunnan after the Tiananmen Square protests. I also know a professor here in Hong Kong who works for the U.S. government. The U.S. is seeking to contact the student leaders at the protests and help them escape to the U.S. If you come to Hong Kong, the professor can arrange political asylum for you in the U.S. Please take down this number and call me when you come to a decision."

"O.K., Zhang,"

After thirty minutes of careful consideration, Chai Ling picked up the handset and dialed back.

"Zhang, I will take the earliest flight to Hong Kong from Kunming tomorrow morning to meet you,"

"Very well, I will meet you at the airport,"

"I will be wearing a blue scarf and a lotus pin," said Chai Ling.

THE NEXT DAY,

The Air China flight from Kunming was prepared to make its descent, circling over Kowloon as the pilot oriented the plane for an approach to the Kai Tak International Airport. By the window seat, Chai Ling looked down at the sprawling Hong Kong metropolis. Chai Ling's first view of the modern city gave her hope away from the repressive regime which she has grown up under as well as the ruthless police who are looking for her.

The plane landed smoothly on the runway alongside the sea on the Kowloon side and Chai Ling began to disembark the plane. She positioned herself in line at immigration control and noticed a man wearing a gray-buttoned shirt and black pants holding a bulky cellular phone in his hand standing ahead of her. Only very few rich businessmen in Hong Kong and China could afford to own ones like that.

Chai Ling cleared immigration control and walked past customs. She emerged into the departure hall and saw a sea of people.

Chang Yen Ci waited by the public telephones with a copy of the South China Morning Post in his arm. He spotted the long-haired, slender Chai Ling and noticed the lotus pin on her scarf.

"You must be Chai Ling, I am Zhang Yen Ci."

"Nihao," said Chai Ling.

"Come with me, we must see Professor Huang Shan Woo right away,"

———

The man with the gray-buttoned shirt dialed the number with his bulky cell phone outside the departure hall.

"Chief Chen, This is Tsai Chin. I have arrived in Hong Kong. The rest of the team are here in Hong Kong. We are prepared to go."

"Good, wait for my instructions," said Chen.

———

The green Kowloon Dik Si picked up Zhang and Chai Ling outside the airport departure hall and made its way to the front of the gate at Lingnan College.

LINGNAN COLLEGE SOCIOLOGY DEPARTMENT L102

The professor was, as always, busy preparing his lessons behind his desk when the two students walked in.

"Professor Woo, I am Chai Ling,"

"Hello, Chai Ling,"

"Nihao, Professor Woo,"

"How was your trip here?"

"I flew from Kunming. The flight was smooth,"

"News reports said that the petition was handed to Premier Zhao Saying. Was that true?"

"Yes, our activists personally handed it to the premier."

"I will send a telegram today to my employer in the U.S. I expect a response tomorrow. Meanwhile, you should get some rest at the hotel and come back tomorrow." said Professor Woo.

"Professor Woo,"

"Yes,"

"I do not want to go to the U.S."

"Where do you want to go?"

"France. I want to go to school and study for my bachelor's there."

———

URGENT WIRE

To: HQ, Langley, Virginia, the United States

From: Red Block, Hong Kong

Contact with student leader Chai Ling today. Chai Ling desires for political asylum in France. Request assistance for diplomatic action to facilitate Chai Ling's passage to France.

———

URGENT WIRE

To: Red Block, Hong Kong

From: HQ, Langley, Virginia, the United States

HQ has secured approval from French government for Chai Ling's passage to France through State Department. Wait for telephone call before bringing Chai Ling to French embassy Hong Kong.

———

Zhang returned to his uncle's house near Victoria peak late at night after dropping off Chai Ling at the Pavilion

Hotel in Causeway Bay on the Hong Kong side. Before going to bed, he looked out of the window from his room on the second storey and saw a blue Datsun parked across the street. Zhang could see two men, one in the driver's seat and the other one on the front passenger seat, smoking a cigarette.

THE NEXT MORNING,

Zhang woke up and finished his green onion pancake for breakfast before grabbing his shoes. He put on a baseball cap and slowly opened the metal gate of his uncle's mansion, taking a peek outside. The blue Datsun was still parked on the same spot as it was last night.

Zhang had already called for a Dik Si and the taxi came right on time. He sprinted out of the metal gate and entered the cab.

"Causeway Bay, Pavilion Hotel," said Zhang to the driver.

The red Dik Si sped past the blue Datsun and continued downhill along the narrow, mountain road, its engine noise awakening the mainland operatives who were asleep in their car. Zhang looked in the rearview mirror from the backseat of the Dik Si and saw the mainland operatives tailing close behind him.

The red Dik Si reached the foothills of Mount Tai Peng and merged into the city traffic towards their destination. Ten minutes later, the car stopped in front of the Pavilion Hotel. Zhang paid the fare, looked behind him as he exited the car, and saw the blue Datsun stopping along the curb one block behind him.

Zhang ran into the hotel lobby and picked up the hotel phone to call Chai Ling.

"Chai Ling, I am here at the hotel lobby. Come down

now. The mainland MSS have found me and they are close behind." said Zhang.

"I will be down there right away," said Chai Ling.

Chai Ling grabbed her luggage, put on her red scarf, and clutched the black address book which contained the phone numbers of the other student leaders in her hand before heading out the door. Without saying a word, Zhang and Chai Ling hurried out of the hotel and hailed a taxi. The red Dik Si came to a screeching halt as the two fugitives jumped in.

From the rearview mirror, Zhang could see another white Toyota pulling in behind the blue Datsun. Inside the blue Datsun, Tsai Chin grabbed his bulky cellular phone.

"Chief, we have spotted Zhang Yen Ci and Chai Ling together. They are in a taxi now. We are following them as we speak."

"Your orders are to capture Chai Ling alive and eliminate Zhang Yen Ci,"

"Yes sir," said Tsai.

The red Dik Si came out of the undersea tunnel and emerged out of the Kowloon side as it made its way towards Lingnan College. The driver took a shortcut heading north and saw the blue Datsun and the white Toyota following close behind.

"There are two cars which have been following us for half an hour now. Are you in any trouble?" the driver said.

"Yes, we got into trouble with the mafia here and they are after us now." said Zhang. "I will pay you more if you can get rid of them."

The driver stepped hard on the pedal as the red Dik Si accelerated to 150 kilometers an hour, zipping past slower traffic. The experienced driver swerved hard as it made a turn to Tun Mun city, losing the blue Datsun. The white Toyota followed Zhang and Chai Ling onto the city streets.

Ten minutes later, the red Dik Si stopped outside the gate of the Lingnan Campus. Zhang paid the extra fare and stepped off with Chai Ling. They sprinted towards the sociology department and looked back; no sight of mainland operatives and the blue Datsun. The two reached L102 and opened the door, finding without surprise, professor Woo sitting behind his desk.

Woo looked up and said in a calm voice.

"I have received the phone call from my employer in the U.S. We must go to the French embassy now. You are scheduled to board the flight tonight to Paris."

"Professor Woo, I'm afraid the situation has gotten worse. The mainland MSS has found us and followed us in their car from Chai Ling's hotel," said Zhang.

"I will borrow a car from the faculty staff and drive you to the French embassy," said the professor.

The white Corolla carrying the two mainland operatives stopped outside the gate of the Lingnan College. One of them picked up a cellular phone.

"Mr. Tsai, we have followed Zhang and Chai Ling to Lingnan College. What are your orders?"

"Kill Zhang as soon as you spot him and bring Chai Ling in alive," said Tsai.

"Yes, sir."

The two mainland operatives, Xiang and Wu, reached for their Red Star pistols and loaded the weapons before stepping out of the car. The two calmly approached the campus gate on foot where they each staked out a spot on opposite sides of the gate.

Professor Woo took the keys from one of his fellow faculty members after promising that nothing would happen to his car and led Zhang and Chai Ling out of the sociology department building towards the adjacent parking structure.

Woo found the yellow Ford Mustang and motioned for Zhang and Chai Ling to step in. The professor had owned an orange Camaro when he was a graduate student in the United States, often taking long road trips from his school in Kentucky to visit his friends in North Carolina. Driving was second nature to him.

Woo pulled out of the parking structure and headed for the campus gate. He pressed hard on the throttle as the yellow Ford Mustang zoomed past the gate, leaving pedestrians and the two mainland operatives behind.

The professor put the yellow Mustang into third gear and quickly moved out the view of the Lingnan College gate and the mainland operatives. Half an hour later, Woo, Zhang, and Chai Ling crossed the undersea tunnel and emerged on the Hong Kong side just a few minutes before 2 p.m. Woo expertly navigated the congested city streets and reached the French embassy, which sat near the sea in Aberdeen on the southern side of Hong Kong island. Built in the 1950's in the classical style, the gray, rectangular building was distinguished by the white columns which adorned the front entrance.

Woo showed his name card to the security guard outside after leaving the car nearby on the street.

"My name is Professor Huang Shan Woo. These are my associates Zhang Yen Ci and Chai Ling. We have an appointment to see the ambassador," said Woo.

"Hold on," said the guard.

The guard looked through the visitor appointment book on the kiosk near his post and found professor Woo's name.

"Come with me."

The guard led Woo, Zhang, and Chai Ling inside the front lobby of the embassy. A French woman dressed in a black suit and wearing a gold necklace approached them.

"Hello, my name is Marie Lidou. I am the embassy's cultural liaison. I will take you to see the ambassador who will get the papers ready for Chai Ling," she said.

Chai Ling looked up and noticed a large chandelier which hung over the front lobby.

"Most of our visitors inside the lobby notice the chandelier first," said Lidou. "It was imported from France and given to the embassy as a gift from a close friend of President Mitterand." said Lidou.

Lidou raised her hand and signaled for the three to follow her. She opened a metal door and took the three along the hallway that was illuminated by a row of windows facing the sea.

A dozen or so fishing boats were moored a few hundred meters from shore and Woo could also make out freighters in the distance sailing the route towards southeast Asia.

The afternoon sun cast a shadow over the floor as the four approached the office of the ambassador's office. Lidou opened the door as the ambassador stood up, obviously impatient to see the faces of the Chinese student leaders who have shocked the world with their act of defiance.

"Hello, Professor Woo, Chai Ling... and this is?"

"This is Zhang Yen Ci. He is an associate of my mine."

"Welcome. Please sit down," said Rison.

"The press have covered the Tiananmen Square protests so extensively that our information section has been kept very busy these past few weeks gathering all the news that has been coming out of Beijing. How is the situation there?" said Rison.

"The situation is chaotic. The PSB are all over the city looking to arrest the demonstrators who were at Tiananmen Square," said Chai Ling.

"I have talked to the officials here in Hong Kong and they all said that this could be a watershed moment that can change China forever." said Rison.

"What do you think, Professor Woo?"

"It is possible that the attention and actions given from the international community can influence future decisions made by the Chinese government. However, it all depends ultimately on the Chinese party leadership." said Woo.

"I hope that this can bring China a step closer to democracy," said Rison.

"We should get on to business," said Rison. "I have here the immigration papers for Chai Ling and a document for Chai Ling to sign for her to relinquish her Chinese citizenship. Chai Ling, the papers must be signed in order for you to attain political asylum in France."

It has been Chai Ling's dream to study in the West and she knew that returning to China would mean certain death.

"I will sign the papers," said Chai Ling.

THE NEXT MORNING,

Zhang Yen Ci woke up early in the morning and poured himself a cup of Oolong tea before sitting down outside the house of Chong I Liang in Sha Tin. He watched as the horizon turned a light orange in the east and heard the scream of the rooster from the farmhouse a few hundred meters away.

Today, he felt satisfied. He had just accomplished a task that would earn him his escape to America and will go meet Professor Woo to receive his immigration papers just as the professor promised.

LINGNAN COLLEGE, SOCIOLOGY DEPARTMENT L102

Professor Woo picked up a copy of the day's South China Morning Post and noticed a sidebar story on the front page with the headline reading: Premier Zhao held under house arrest: report.

He continued reading the story.

"Chinese premier Zhao Zhiyang has been put under house arrest somewhere in Beijing for siding with the student leaders during the Tiananmen Square protests a week ago, according to sources close to the party leadership.

A handful of members from the Standing Committee of the PRC Communist Party opposed premier Zhao's handling of the Tiananmen Square situation as it came to a close during the committee's close door meetings.

Those members decided to place premier Zhao under house arrest as punishment for his views that had been deemed too radical for the establishment, a source close to the leadership told the Post.

Premier Zhao personally received a petition from the student leaders of the Tiananmen Square protests last which week which called for democratic reforms."

Professor Woo put down the newspaper and looked out his office window. The opportunity had come to reach out to Premier Zhao, his primary mission objective. At ten a.m. Zhang Yen Ci arrived with Professor Woo behind his desk reading his student's assignments. The professor looked up and gave a stern look.

"Zhang, I'm afraid there has been a change of plans. My employer in the U.S. has ordered me to make contact with Premier Zhao Ziyang. The morning newspaper this morning ran a story which said that the premier has been placed under house arrest somewhere in Beijing. I need you to ask your father where the premier is being held as well as help me to reach Zhao. Until I obtain his help, I cannot assist you with your political asylum process."

"But you promised me before that I can escape to the U.S. once I bring Chai Ling to you."

"Plans have changed, Zhang. My employer will not go forward in assisting you unless you help me on this mission," said Woo.

"Okay, I will make a phone call to my father this morning,"

Zhang stepped out of the campus and walk towards the public phone booth on the sidewalk. Assured that no one was following him, he entered and dialed the number to his father's house.

"Hello," Zhang Shan Yen said.

"Father, this is Yen Ci. Professor Woo needs to know where Premier Zhao is being kept in Beijing. He said he will assist me to escape to the U.S. if you help him reach premier Zhao."

"I understand. I will help him." said Shan Yen.

Three days later,

The Air China flight from Hong Kong to Beijing landed safely at Beijing Capital Airport at exactly 11:20 a.m. in the morning, leaving enough time for professor Woo to meet Zhang Shan Yen and enjoy their scheduled lunch.

The city of the Forbidden City has been locked against outside influence from within ever since the emperor Zhu Di decided to move the capital here from the south in 1402. Peking, the name of the city that was first known to western invaders who had taken over the ports and destroyed the nearby Summer Palace of the Qing emperor in 1860, had always been a distant, unfamiliar name located at the end of the Silk Road trade route.

Professor Woo was met at the airport arrivals hall by

Zhang Shan Yen, who was wearing a white dress shirt and blue trousers. He had come alone and had made sure that no PSB or MSS people were following him.

"Hello, Professor Woo,"

"Hello, General Zhang,"

"Come with me. We shall have lunch first and then I will bring you to see premier Zhao." said Zhang.

General Zhang Shan Yen took the lead and showed Professor Woo to his private Cadillac parked along the curb outside. He took the wheel of the Cadillac with the professor in the passenger seat and sped off towards Beijing proper. Zhang turned onto the airport expressway and cruised at the speed limit of 85 kilometers an hour. The summer clouds trapped the heat from the sun and created heavy smog that hovered over Beijing on this particular day.

"Is this your first time in Beijing?"

"Yes, it is,"

"I will take you to Quanjude restaurant at Wangfujing for Peking Duck. The best in town," Zhang chuckled as he said.

The sun came directly over head as the Cadillac exited the airport expressway and turned onto the second ring road just a little after noon. Before long, Zhang and professor Woo reached Jianguomenwai Dajie and drove past the ancient observatory. Soon after, the majestic sight of the south wall of the Forbidden City came into view on the right with the expansive Tiananmen Square directly across to the left. The public square had been cordoned off on all sides and Woo saw charred marks left behind by the fires from two weeks ago that remained on the concrete.

Ten minutes later, Zhang and Woo reached the bustling commercial district of Wangfujing. The pedestrian walkway that cut through the center of the district was lined by shops and restaurants.

Zhang and Woo stopped into the restaurant and ordered the three-course Peking Duck lunch which came with the roast-marinated duck with sweet sauce and buns, Beef with Peking Sauce, and the Kung Pao Chicken.

"Do you want to drink a beer?"

"No," said Woo.

"Professor Woo, I envy you. You live in a modern city and enjoy all the freedoms that we don't have here. Deng Xiaoping has been trying hard to turn the country around after Mao Zedong and frankly I have seen too much strife and turmoil suffered by the people.

"With that to say, I admit that Deng's reform policies are a step in the right direction. The special economic zone of Shenzhen has developed quickly into a manufacturing hub with help from the rich businessmen in Hong Kong just an hour train ride away."

"Beijing has been changing rather slowly," the general continued. Perhaps it is because this is the power center of China and pressure on officials to maintain stability has hindered development in the city," said the general. "I am really disappointed at the pace of reforms,"

"Maybe this Tiananmen Square protest is a good thing," Woo said in a suggestive tone. "It will give the government a big jolt and the people awareness to the plight that is facing the nation."

"I have seen the poverty in the villages and small towns of the countryside. It is time that people wake up and become aware of the rampant corruption that happens in all levels of government. The communist system does not encourage people to work for a reward and this will lead to more people seeking the easier way out to get ahead; by bribing their officials when they want to buy a house, a car, or to start a Ke Ti Hu business."

Professor Woo gave a slight nod and paused, putting down his chopsticks. The restaurant was full of patrons and the clamor filled the establishment with a sense of excitement. Peking duck was the main order on every table and this place on Wangfujing has enjoyed hundreds of years of history as the one carrying the authentic taste.

After finishing their meals, Zhang walked to the public phone outside the restaurant and placed a call to Major Wang. Wang has served alongside Zhang for decades in the PLA and has become a close friend and confidante of Zhang. Zhang had already planned for Wang to drive him and Professor Woo to see Premier Zhao.

The streets of Wangfujing were clogged with a sea of pedestrians and provided the perfect cover for this secret operation. There is a Chinese saying, "The most obviously dangerously place is the safest place."

"Wang, I am here with Professor Woo at Wangfujing Peking Duck restaurant. You can come now."

"I will be behind schedule. There are two PSB patrol cars outside my house right now. The word of your secret meeting probably has been leaked. I will call your pager once I know I am safe."

The major hung up.

Major Wang approached the window and looked outside of his house. Four plain clothes policeman were sitting inside the patrol cars reading the latest issue of the People's Daily. Wang went into his bedroom and changed into a blue dress shirt and black pants. The traditional courtyard residence which Wang live in featured, like many others, a back gate. Wang picked up his briefcase and slipped out the backdoor. He rushed towards his black

BMW that was parked on a dirt lot adjacent to his house and stepped in.

Major Wang started the engine and pulled out into the paved road, setting his course for the East Asia World shopping center in Wangfujing. Ten minutes later, he arrived inside the parking garage of the shopping mall and chose a dark corner space where he parked. Wang stepped out and walked on foot to the telephone booth on the ground floor of the shopping mall. He dialed the number to Zhang's pager and waited. Five minutes later, the phone rang and Wang picked up.

"Wang, Where are you right now?"

"I'm at the East Asia shopping center just ten minutes away from your restaurant?"

"Are you being followed?"

"No. I will meet you at the restaurant in my car in ten minutes."

Wang hung up the telephone and took a look around him. No sign of police.

Two minutes later, the major was back inside his black BMW. Wang started the engine and drove the BMW to the Peking Duck restaurant which was just around the block. Making sure he was not being followed, Wang made the final turn and stopped just outside the restaurant where Zhang and Professor Woo stood.

"We will make it to premier Zhao Ziyang's residence in about thirty minutes," said Wang.

"Only a handful of high-ranking officers in the military know where Zhao is being held," said Zhang. "When we pass the guards, Professor Woo, remember to say that you are an information officer who we have brought in to interrogate the premier."

"I will remember that," said Professor Woo.

The black BMW swept past Jianguomenwai Dajie and turned into a quiet neighborhood in Zhaoyang District. Wang stopped the car in front of the gate of a traditional courtyard residence guarded on all sides by an eight-foot high stone wall.

Two PLA soldiers armed with rifles stood guard in front of the gate. The guards immediately recognized Zhang and saluted.

"At ease," said Zhang.

"How is the premier?" said Zhang.

"The premier is taking his afternoon nap right now."

"I am here with major Wang and information officer lieutenant Chin to interrogate the premier on the details of the Tiananmen Square protests."

"Yes, sir."

The two guards led the group into the house where they were told to wait in the living room. The house was an old residence that used to belong to a member of the Politburo, the body that rules over the major policy decisions of the nation.

One of the guards entered into the bedroom and woke the premier.

"Premier Zhao, General Zhang is here to see you. He is with an information officer who wants to ask you some questions."

The premier put on his glasses, adjusted his robe, and walked out into the living room where Zhang, Wang, and Professor Woo stood waiting. Zhang signaled for the two guards to step outside.

"Premier, this is Professor Woo from Hong Kong. He has some matters to discuss with you," said Zhang.

"Hello, professor Woo,"

"Hello, premier Zhao. I have an important message from

the U.S. government that I am bringing to you. The U.S. is concerned on your well-being after the Tiananmen Square protests. They wish to know if you have any intentions of perhaps taking refuge in the United States. If so, the U.S. government is willing to offer you political asylum."

"I will consider this carefully," said Premier Zhao. "Thank you."

Professor Woo reached into his pocket and took out a key, placing it on the table in front of Zhao.

"This is a key to a mailbox in Beijing which you can use to send communication to me in Hong Kong. Here is my name card."

CHAPTER 7

Inside the Wat Phra Thong temple in southern Thailand, thirty monks dressed in golden-laced robes knelt in front of the Buddha statue and entered their chants in the most devout Buddhist nation in the world. The temple carried a little known secret that no other temple has: a tooth relic of the Bodhisattva that had been passed from temple to temple throughout the centuries from India.

Towards the end of their chant, the head of the temple stepped into the prayer hall and sounded the gong. The thirty monks rose and found chairs to sit, taking a break from the two hour long prayer session that was performed on a daily basis.

The head of the temple signaled for the group's attention in the middle of the hall.

"Fellow monks, I have a message to bring you. The Fokuangshan monastery in Taiwan has offered a donation to us in exchange for the tooth relic that we currently own. After a discussion with our other monks, we have decided to accept the offer. The representatives from Fokuangshan will arrive here next week for the transfer."

Solomon had been on numerous flights from Los Angeles

to Taipei, but this time it was different. He had plans on working in Taiwan after seeing the economic growth that the country has experienced in the past decade. He also wanted to get away from Winnie and all the memories that they shared in Los Angeles.

Solomon had already made arrangements to stay in the home of Michael Wei's younger brother Joshua while he looked for a job in Taipei. A room was available on the rooftop of the three story building while Joshua, his wife Theresa, and their ten-year-old daughter stayed on the third floor.

After picking up his luggage at the baggage claim, Solomon stepped out of the arrivals gate where he met with Joshua Wei and his wife Theresa. Putting two bags – all of Solomon's belongings -- inside the trunk of Joshua Wei's Toyota Tercel, Wei then drove off towards his new home in Taipei.

"What kind of job are you looking for?" asked Wei as the Tercel sped along the Sun Yat Sen freeway to Taipei.

"Any job in the field of communications," said Solomon.

Joshua Wei and Theresa's home was located on Xinhai Road right across from the campus of Taiwan's most prestigious university, National Taiwan University. The basketball courts on the campus were popular for competitive pickup basketball matches which Solomon had played in when he was younger.

One of the impressions that Solomon gained from his numerous visits to Taiwan in the 1990's was the changing role of the woman in society. Rising from the traditional Chinese role of the humble housewife, more Taiwan women were gaining important positions in big corporations and in government.

Theresa Wei was the perfect example of the Chinese

woman in the new Taiwan society. Graduating with a bachelor's degree in Taiwan's prestigious National Chengchi University, she went on to complete her master's degree in communications at Michigan State University. Upon her return to Taiwan, she attained the position of the director of public relations for Taiwan's largest domestic cable TV station, Videoland, Inc.

On his visit to Taiwan the previous year, Solomon was given an intern position by Theresa Wei at Videoland, Inc. Solomon was given the job of assembling media kits of the new programming which were to be passed out to Taiwan's media outlets.

Solomon planned on pursuing a career in the field of communications and returning to the United States after one or two years to build experience for his future career.

After the R.O.C. government lifted martial law in 1987, restrictions on the freedom of press in Taiwan were eliminated and newspapers, magazines, radio stations, and TV stations proliferated.

The three major newspapers in Taiwan are the China Times, United Daily News, and the pro-independence Liberty Times. The government-owned Central News Agency provided news with the official slant to Taiwan's newspapers and TV and radio news broadcasters.

One week after Solomon's arrival in Taiwan, Theresa Wei invited Solomon to a company party at a karaoke parlor in Taipei. Solomon accepted the invitation and received a first-hand taste of Taiwan's guanxi culture, where business is mixed indiscriminately with personal relationships.

Two English newspapers offered their daily dishing to the foreign expatriate population in Taiwan, albeit with different political perspectives: The China Courier and the pro-independence Taiwan Herald.

Within two weeks after he began his search, Solomon landed an interview with Reuters news agency which was seeking reporters. Solomon's job interview with Reuters went well until the end when the interviewer asked him how long he would stay in Taiwan. Solomon told the truth, saying that he would stay at most two years. The Reuters interviewer pressed Solomon to stay for five years at which Solomon stood up and walked out of the office.

―――――

At the end of his one month stay with Joshua Wei, Solomon knew that he was outstaying his welcome and he moved out to a room near the National Taiwan Normal University.

Right after moving into his new room, Solomon received a phone call from his uncle who was working in a Taiwan computer company. The two agreed to meet at a restaurant near Solomon's place. At the restaurant, Solomon's uncle asked him if he needed help in his job search. Solomon refused his uncle's offer for help and said that he would be able to find a job by himself.

At his new place, Solomon found out that one of his housemates, Peter Hart was also a graduate of UCLA and that his ex-girlfriend was a graduate of the high school which Solomon attended. An engineering student at UCLA, Hart was studying Chinese at the Mandarin Training Center at National Taiwan Normal University.

Solomon's other housemates were also foreigners studying Chinese in Taipei, including Aaron Gomez from Texas and Assaf from Israel. The four of them would often go out to the bars on weekends and have a few drinks. The DV8 became a favorite haunt for the four.

―――――

On Chinese New Year, when most of the stores and of-
fices across the country shut down, Solomon, Gomez, and
Assaf set off on a trip to the scenic Alishan, a mountain
resort in the central part of the island. The three took the
long-distance bus from Taipei to Chiayi City, where they connected to the Alishan Rail Line for the three and half hour
trip to Alishan. All agreed that the countryside was where
the true beauty of Taiwan lies as the train took the three
housemates from lush tropical forests to the high mountains of Taiwan's Central Mountain Range.

The three housemates checked in at the hotel on the eve
of Chinese New Year and reserved a room for two nights.
The next morning, Solomon, Gomez, and Assaf joined the
throngs of Taiwan citizens on what has become a ritual
of visiting Alishan, the witnessing of the sunrise over the
Central Mountain Range from Chushan.

Solomon, Gomez, and Assaf decided to take on the
day-long hike descending from Alishan to the Shan Lin Hsi
recreation area where they would take the bus to Taipei.
The trail that started at Alishan's Monkey Rock led its way
through abandoned tunnels and across numerous ravines
before connecting to a dirt road. It was dark when Solomon,
Gomez, and Assaf reached an eight-foot-high fence guarding one of the entrances to the Shan Lin Hshi recreation
area. The three then hurled themselves over.

———

One week later, Solomon landed a job interview with
The China Courier. At the newsroom, Solomon was given a
test translating a Chinese news article into English. Solomon
took twenty minutes to finish translating the article.

Solomon was given a two-month trial period during which he would work at the national desk reading over stories from the news wires and translating before he could go out on assignments.

Solomon agreed to take the job and started working the next day.

A month and a half into the trial period, editor Jason Jones gave Solomon his first assignment. The story was on the government's failed Romanization of Chinese road signs which created much confusion for westerners in Taiwan. Solomon interviewed a professor at Taiwan's government-funded research institution Academia Sinica for his analysis of the flaws of Taiwan's Romanization system. Part of the problem, according to the professor, was Taiwan's mixed use of the Wade Giles system and the Pinyin system which was used in mainland China.

Three weeks later, a story on a Buddha finger bone arriving in Taiwan in the Chinese newspaper The China Times caught Solomon's eye. According to the news article, one of Buddha's last remaining finger bones which was kept in a temple in Thailand would be brought over to Taiwan to be worshipped by Buddhists on April 29, 1998.

Solomon asked the editor if he could have the story. Given the go-ahead, Solomon wrote his first article with a byline which appeared on the front page on April 23.

The article read:

Buddha relic to be brought to Taiwan

By Solomon Woo

Buddhist master Hsin Hua will set out on a mission to bring one of Buddhism's most sacred relics, the Buddha's finger bone, to Taiwan to stay.

One of the Buddha's last remaining finger bones is being kept in a monastery in Thailand and will be given to Taiwan as a gift, said Buddhist master Hsin Hua yesterday.

Hsin Hua will travel to Thailand tomorrow to attend the handover of the holy relic which will be received at the Chiang Kai Shek International Airport in Taipei on Wednesday with a Buddhist ritual.

One day after the article ran, Solomon came in to the newsroom prepared to write a story on Taiwan's preparations for the Buddha finger bone in Taipei when the editor approached him with a pile of papers.

"Here are the reports on the Buddha finger bone story which the wire services ran today," said the editor. "The wires have picked up your story. You can look it over. By the way, mainland China Xinhua also has a report."

The Xinhua story ran on mainland China's official newspapers and questioned the authenticity of the Buddha finger bone that was slated to arrive in Taiwan.

Solomon's story had gone "international," and Solomon was feeling the attention that his story garnered.

The day before the finger bone's scheduled arrival in Taipei, Solomon went to the library of the National Taiwan Normal University in Taipei to research his subject. Solomon came upon a book on the history of the Buddha relic in China and checked it out.

———

The day of the Buddha relic's arrival in Taiwan, Solomon came to Chiang Kai-shek International Airport one hour early after a forty-minute bus ride from Taipei. A stage was set up inside the hangar at the airport to receive the Buddha relic once it arrives via a China Airlines flight from Thailand. Solomon noticed a team of western journalists near the stage.

The next day, Solomon's story appeared on the front page of The China Courier:

Buddha relic welcomed in ancient ritual

By Solomon Woo

Thousands of devout Buddhists welcomed the arrival of the much-awaited finger bone relic of the Buddha to Taiwan yesterday with religious celebrations and a ritual dating back to Tang Dynasty China.

Led by Master Hsin Hua, the relic arrived at Chiang Kai-shek International Airport onboard a special China Airlines flight from Thailand where the finger bone had been presented to the Buddhist master by monks from a Buddhist monastery.

Government officials said during the ceremony that the Buddha's finger bone offered Taiwan citizens hope and peace for the future before the relic was escorted to Taipei where it was paraded along the streets before worshippers.

In ancient China around one thousand A.D., the Buddha's finger bone was ordered by the devout Buddhist Tang Emperor to be moved to the imperial city of Xian just as the emperor's predecessors had done to ensure peace and prosperity to his nation.

Crowds lined the streets of Xian to receive the Buddha relic which entered the city in a procession comprised of monks and nuns.

The most peaceful and culturally flourishing period in Chinese history happened to come about while the Tang emperors practiced this tradition.

One thousand years later in Taiwan, the scene was repeated as worshippers crowded the streets in Taipei to receive the Buddha's finger bone. Government officials speaking at the ceremony expressed hope that the nation would prosper like the Tang era.

———

Two days later, the New York Times ran a small piece that appeared on the world section under the headline "Taiwan places faith in Buddha's finger bone," leading with mainland China's questioning of the Buddha relic's authenticity.

———

On May 1, 1998, head of National Security Bureau's operations division Tung Liang received a phone call from NSB chief Hao Chien-kuo ordering Tung to place a wire tap at Solomon's home.

———

CHAPTER 8

Two weeks after Solomon's Buddha finger bone article ran, publisher Jack Hsiao called Solomon to his office on a rainy Monday morning. Solomon entered Hsiao's office on the seventh floor where Hsiao signaled Cheng to sit down.

"Your two-month trial period is almost over," said Hsiao. "We have decided to keep you on the job. What particular subjects are you interested in?"

"I like sports," said Solomon.

"O.K. sports editor Jeffrey Wilcox has been requesting for more help at the sports desk," said Hsiao. "Starting to-morrow, you will work under him as an assistant.

———

Solomon's first assignment at the sports desk came two days before the start of the World Cup in France on June 10, 1998. Solomon was given the task of reporting the Taipei bar scene which was filled with expatriates watching the World Cup.

Wilcox was able to secure a sponsor deal with Dominoes Pizza for the newspaper's coverage of the World Cup. The China Courier would print discount coupons of the pizza company in the sports section which could be validated by the reader after he or she answers sports trivia questions.

The China Courier also had a correspondent at the World Cup who would file stories back to Wilcox.

———

Solomon saved up enough money in July, 1998 to move from his old room to a one-bedroom apartment atop a residential building in the affluent Ta An district. The apartment has a partial view of Ta-An Park, Taipei's largest city park, from the bedroom window.

There was a cable TV line that ran across the water tower adjacent to Solomon's apartment, and he was able to extend the line into his own apartment.

Taiwan's myriad of cable TV channels included four local news channels and programming from the U.S. such as CNN, ESPN, and Discovery. Solomon spent much of the day keeping up to date on sports news and general news before he went to work at four in the afternoon.

In the end of July, Solomon decided to give Joshua and Theresa Wei a call.

"Hi, Joshua," said Solomon.

"Hi, Solomon. Long time no hear." said Joshua Wei.

"Let's go out for dinner," said Solomon. "I heard the buffet restaurant at the Hilton Hotel is good! My treat. You can tell Theresa to come, too."

"O.K.," said Joshua Wei. "When?"

"Tomorrow at six," said Solomon.

The next day, Joshua and Theresa Wei arrived outside the Hilton buffet restaurant five minutes before Solomon. The waiter led the three to a table with a view of a garden terrace.

"So where are you working now?" said Theresa Wei.

"I am working at The China Courier," said Solomon. "I am an assistant editor at the sports desk."

"So, how is work at Videoland?" said Solomon.

"There have been several people laid off at the company," said Theresa Wei. "They were laid off with salary paid. People are afraid that they may be next."

———

In September, Solomon was given an assignment to cover the annual R. William Jones Cup international basketball tournament in Taipei, the biggest international basketball tournament in Taipei. The big story was the entry of Philippine Centennial basketball team which consisted of all-stars from the Philippines professional basketball league PBA.

Taiwan was also represented by a selection of all-stars from its own professional basketball league Chinese Basketball Association. The host nation must play under the designation "Chinese Taipei" as part of an arrangement with the International Olympic Committee after protests by mainland China more than a decade ago.

Chinese Taipei and Philippines were considered the favorites entering the tournament and the Philippine Centennial team was expected to attract a large following of the Filipino foreign workers in Taiwan.

As expected, Chinese Taipei and Philippines met at the final after the end of group play. Solomon was surprised to see exactly half of the Taipei Physical Education Gymnasium filled with Filipino fans, whose cheers almost drowned out that of the local crowd.

———

The Philippine Centennial team outplayed Chinese Taipei 82-72 and won the title of R. William Jones Cup champion.

———

Solomon's work every day at The China Courier included reading the wire, suggesting wire stories to the sports editor to be included on the sports page, and occasionally doing the write-up for the daily Chinese Professional Baseball League games. Stories which Solomon reported from the field include NBA basketball players' visits to Taiwan, the Tour de Taiwan bicycle race, and the Hualien County triathlon.

The China Courier readership included foreign expatriates and their families, ambassadors and official representatives, as well as foreign students learning Chinese.

On a slow news day, Wilcox would send Solomon to report on the Taipei American School's sports competitions against local high schools and international high schools across Southeast Asia.

———

JUNE 10, 1992

Sisy Liu returned to Taiwan after quitting her graduate studies at UC Berkeley. Her parents and DPP legislator Su Wen-ying whom Liu helped elect to office greeted her at Chiang Kai-shek International Airport.

At dinner that night, Su suggested that Liu run for the legislature which was dominated by the Kuomintang. Su said that Liu can run on her wide family connections with the pro-Taiwan independence DPP as well his support.

One month later, Liu announced her candidacy as a DPP legislator for Ilan County and opened her campaign office in the county's largest city Luotong.

After an intensive, four-month campaign, Liu was elected to the Legislature over a young, inexperienced Kuomintang candidate. After the 1992 elections, the Kuomintang maintained its dominance in the Legislature with 103 seats over the DPP's 50 seats.

CHAPTER 9

MARCH 20, 1999

U.S.-led NATO launched an airstrike on Yugoslavia after diplomatic efforts failed to broker a cease-fire agreement between government forces and rebel militias in the region of Kosovo.

Solomon watched CNN during the weeks leading up to the airstrike and became abhorred by the one-sided coverage given against Yugoslavia government and its leader Slobodan Milosevic.

The bombings by US-led NATO against Yugoslavia received wide coverage in the international press and China Courier's international desk editors gave extended coverage to the Kosovo war as well based on wire services.

One month later, sports editor Wilcox came to Solomon's desk in the newsroom on the fifth floor of The China Courier building.

"The organizer of the Chinese Taipei Ice Hockey League (CTIHL) has sent me an e-mail on a potential story," said Wilcox. "He thought that we may be interested in doing an interview on a Yugoslavia player in the league. Here is the organizer's name and phone number."

One day later, Solomon called the CTIHL organizer and obtained the Yugoslav player's name and phone number.

Solomon called Milo Karadjordjevic from the newsroom and scheduled an interview at a restaurant in Taichung two days later. Karadjordjevic said that he would pick up Solomon at the Taichung train station.

The day of the interview, Karadjordjevic drove up to the train station in a white Datsun and greeted Solomon politely.

"Hop in," said Karadjordjevic.

"So how long have you been living in Taichung?"

"Two years," said Karadjordjevic. "I like it here. On weekends, I would go bicycling with my friends at Tunghai University."

Solomon and Karadjordjevic arrived at a Szechuan restaurant in downtown Taichung and sat down near the window. Solomon took out his tape recorder and notebook and put them on the table.

The first question Solomon asked was Karadjordjevic's view of the Yugoslavia war. Solomon followed it up with questions on Karadjordjevic's play in the Chinese Taipei Ice Hockey League and his team's results.

The interview lasted thirty minutes and Solomon said goodbye to Karadjordjevic before taking a taxi to the train station.

The following day, Solomon came in to The China Courier newsroom and finished writing the story. With Wilcox away on vacation, Solomon handed his story over to the copy editors and edited the sports page that day.

APRIL 22, 1999

Solomon's Yugoslav ice hockey player story appeared on the sports page of The China Courier:

Yugoslav ice hockey champion hopes end to war

By Solomon

Yugoslavia-born Milo Karadjordjevic of the Chinese Taipei Ice Hockey League champion Taichung

Canucks called on the U.S. government and its NATO allies to end its airstrikes on Yugoslavia.

Karadjordjevic said yesterday that the invasion of his home country by U.S.-led NATO must stop.

The CTIHL champion said that he has been in touch with his family in Yugoslavia every couple of days this past month and that NATO bombing had fortunately steered away from his hometown of Nis.

U.S.-led NATO began bombing Yugoslavia over one month ago in a pre-emptive attack on the sovereign nation after civil war broke out in the Yugoslav region of Kosovo. The U.S. had failed to broker a peace agreement.

Night fell as Solomon began editing the sports page in the newsroom with Wilcox still away on vacation. Stories from North America usually came in over the wire during the day, but Solomon must wait until late at night for stories coming in from Europe.

Reading the wire and selecting stories took the longest time. Solomon would then send his stories to the copy editors who would give the edited stories to the page designers. Solomon would then select photos off the wire service and present them to the page designers.

Solomon looked over the final layout which the page designers printed out for him and signed off on the sheet at 12 a.m.

The last bus for Ta-an Park leaves at 12:30 a.m. three blocks away from The China Courier building and Solomon hurried along his way to the bus stop on Minsheng West Road.

Solomon made the 12:30 bus and a half an hour

later arrived at Ta-An Park where he would begin the long walk home. In the darkness, Solomon for the first time felt a fear for his own life. Despite his worries, Solomon told himself that he was working on the side of justice and pressed on.

———

The second night after the Yugoslav ice hockey player story ran Solomon returned home from work at 1 a.m. as usual. Solomon took a shower and watched the news until two a.m. when he went to bed.

Five minutes into his sleep Solomon began to notice the sound of a helicopter flying over his apartment. The helicopter flew away and Solomon fell asleep.

The next night, the helicopter flew again over Solomon's apartment as he was trying to go to sleep. This time, Solomon could hear the helicopter well into the early morning and the noise now affected his sleep. For the next three days, the helicopter repeatedly flew over Solomon's place late at night and created noise that lasted into the early morning.

———

The smog lingering over the Taipei basin choked Solomon's senses as he began to seek a solution to the problem. Through the phone book, Solomon found a private investigator and placed the call to the P.I from a public phone near his apartment.

———

"I think that my apartment is being watched," said Solomon. "I want to know what you can do to help."

"We can do a sweep of your apartment using my transmitter detectors," said the private investigator. When do you want me to come?"

"Can you come right now?" said Solomon.

Two hours later, the private investigator knocked on the door of Solomon's apartment.

The private investigator immediately pulled out his transmitter detector from his bag and pointed it at the walls around Solomon's bedroom. He then entered the living room and repeated the same action.

"I can't get a signal," said the private investigator. "Your apartment is clear. Do you want me to check on your phone line?"

"O.K." said Solomon.

"I found something," said the P.I.

He placed the bug on Solomon's table.

Solomon was shocked as he saw the private investigator lay the device on the table.

"Do you want me to install a surveillance protection unit on your phone line?

"How much would it cost?" said Solomon.

"A top-of-the-line surveillance protection machine would cost you NT$15,000."

"No," said Solomon.

———

MAY 7, 1999

U.S.-led NATO had expanded its bombing campaign beyond Kosovo to include targets in the Yugoslavia capital Belgrade. Relying on intel by the CIA, a U.S. bomber launched an airstrike on the Chinese embassy in Belgrade and killed three Chinese reporters inside.

Immediately after the strike on the Chinese embassy, the Chinese ambassador to the United Nations phoned his U.S. counterpart in the wee hours of the morning and called for an emergency U.N. Security Council meeting.

The hit on the Chinese embassy was later determined to be a mistake on the part of the CIA, which claimed that it mistook the Chinese embassy for a Yugoslav logistics warehouse.

Riled by the deadly missile strike, thousands of Chinese held a protest outside the U.S. embassy in Beijing and expressed their anger at western journalists who were present covering the civil unrest. Anger over the strike quickly spread across the country as far south as Guangzhou where thousands took to the streets to voice their contempt against the U.S.

President Clinton subsequently apologized for the incident and promised monetary compensation for the family of the victims who lost their lives in Belgrade.

One month later, continuous bombing by U.S.-led NATO forced Yugoslav president Slobodan Milosevic to surrender and withdraw all Yugoslav troops out of Kosovo. Milosevic also allowed the presence of international peacekeepers into the war-torn region.

JUNE, 1999

Solomon was watching television in his apartment after work when he received a call on his cell phone.

"Hello, is this Solomon," a man's voice sounded over the line.

"Yes," said Solomon.

"This is Greg Chang! How are you?" said Chang.

"I am doing well. Where are you?" said Solomon.

"I am in Taipei right now," said Chang. "I got your number from your aunt. Let's get together some time."

"O.K. There is a Japanese barbecue restaurant near my apartment," said Solomon. "I'll meet you at the northeast corner of Ta-An Park and we'll walk to the restaurant."

The next day, Solomon and Chang sat down at the Japanese barbecue restaurant and the two talked. Chang had been working at a software company in Taipei for two months.

Solomon refrained from divulging his phone bug discovery to Chang, one of his best friends, and kept quiet for the rest of the night. The two left the restaurant and said goodbye.

———

JULY 5, 1999

Solomon was eating dinner at the cafeteria outside the newsroom when Wilcox walked in and took a seat.

"I want to let you know that I will be quitting in August," said Wilcox. "I already notified Hsiao. "I don't know what Hsiao's arrangement for you would be."

Wilcox stood up and returned to his desk in the newsroom.

Two days later, Hsiao called Solomon to the conference room.

"Wilcox is quitting in August," said Hsiao. "We want you to fill his position as sports editor. I expect you to produce the best English-language sports page in town," said Hsiao.

"O.K." said Solomon.

———

JULY 9, 1999

The lead story on the front page of The China Courier was President Lee Teng-hui's explanation of the cross-strait relationship as a "special state-to-state relationship" during an interview with German news service Deutsche Welle.

"The 1991 constitutional amendments have designated cross-strait relations as a state-to-state relationship or at least a special state-to-state relationship, rather than an internal relationship between a legitimate government and a renegade group, or between a central government and a local government," Lee said.

Lee's definition of relations between Taiwan and mainland China created controversy within the island and prompted a backlash from the PRC.

Mainland China's official news service Xinhua quoted top mainland officials who criticized Lee for his indiscriminate comments while labeling him as a reviled figure keen on advocating Taiwan independence.

A respected leader as president and as Kuomintang chairman who moved the nation along the path of democracy for the latter part of the twentieth century, Lee marked the beginning of Kuomintang's downfall with his faulty explanation of the fragile relationship between the Republic of China and the People's Republic of China.

———

AUGUST 6, 1999

For the second year in a row, Solomon was assigned to cover the R. William Jones Cup basketball tournament in Taipei. This year, the Philippines was represented by an all-star team selected from the country's secondary professional league. Facing the Philippine team in early group play, Chinese Taipei returned to the tournament with much of the same players as last year. Tempers flared early in the Philippine-Chinese Taipei game with the Philippine team committing hard fouls early. The crowd inside the Taipei Physical Education Gymnasium booed every time the Philippine players would earn a technical. A hard kick to the knee of Chinese Taipei star player Cheng Chih-lung by a Philippine player finally angered the onlookers as plastic bottles and beverage containers flew onto the court, hitting a number of Philippine players and narrowly missing Solomon. The referee stopped the game and tournament organizers Chinese Taipei Basketball League appealed for calm in a news conference after the game.

———

AUGUST 10, 1999

On the same day when Solomon assumed the position as sports editor he decided to divulge his secret to the publisher. Solomon waited until the time when Hsiao usually came to the building and approached managing editor Lai.

"I want to have a meeting with the publisher," said Solomon.

"Let me call to see if he is in his office," said Lai.

Moments later, Solomon was told to meet with the publisher at his office on the seventh floor. Solomon climbed up two stories to the seventh floor and found Hsiao's office.

Solomon knocked on the door.

"Come in," said Hsiao.

Hsiao was sitting behind a desk as Solomon was told to sit down.

"I discovered a wiretap on my phone at home," said Solomon. "I just want to let you know."

"O.K. You may go now," said Hsiao.

SEPTEMBER 20, 1999

Solomon punched his timecard and left The China Courier building as usual thirty minutes before midnight. He caught the last bus heading to Ta-An Park and returned to his apartment at 12:30 a.m. After taking a shower, Solomon watched CNN in the living room until one hour later when disaster befell Taiwan. At 1:19 a.m., September 21 an earthquake hit Taiwan and knocked out the power at Solomon's apartment. The shaking continued for two minutes and Solomon, living on the top floor of the apartment building, felt the apartment swaying the hardest. After the shaking subsided, Solomon gathered his strength and ventured out of his apartment to check if the rest of the building lost power. On the rooftop overlooking the cityscape, Solomon saw the entire city as well as his apartment building completely blacked out.

The earthquake registered 7.2 on the Richter scale and the Central Weather Bureau announced the epicenter as near the center of Taiwan in the county of Nantou. More than two thousand lives were lost in central Taiwan as a result of collapsed buildings in the costliest natural disaster ever to hit Taiwan.

Taipei was spared of major damages with the exception of one commercial building that had collapsed due in part to faulty construction.

OCTOBER, 1999

Liu served out her second term as a legislator for the Democratic Progressive Party and accepted a job offer from a radio station to work as a host for a talk show. Liu had earned a reputation as an intelligent yet feisty legislator who seldom feared to air out her criticisms against the Kuomintang.

Liu's radio talk show received high ratings and the former National Security Bureau operative soon received offers to host a talk show on cable television.

CHAPTER 10

DECEMBER, 1999

Campaign for the presidency in Taiwan began in earnest pitting vice president Lien Chan and running mate Premier Vincent Siew of the Kuomintang against Taipei mayor Chen Shui-bian and his running mate Taoyuan County chief Annette Lu of the Democratic Progressive Party.

Despite repeated stumping of the Kuomintang candidates by Lee, polls showed public distrust of Kuomintang as more than the DPP candidates. Speculation by local media that Lee was secretly supporting the DPP further eroded public confidence in the Kuomintang.

Missing a clear political platform and caricatures, the Kuomintang candidates relied on the support of President Lee as its only campaign strategy rather than mobilizing its grassroots supporters, leaving the party out of touch with the public.

Three months before the presidential elections, a rift appeared within Kuomintang when former provincial governor James Soong declared his candidacy for the president as an independent. The move proved divisive within the ranks of the Kuomintang as the party expelled Soong and more than thirty members in the KMT for supporting him.

Hurt by the loss, the Kuomintang filed a suit against Soong for embezzling funds during his tenure as the Kuomintang secretary-general under then president and chairman Chiang Ching-kuo.

Polls had shown Soong leading immediately following his announcement of his candidacy for president. But the lawsuit against Soong harmed his image and dropped him behind DPP's Chen in the polls.

Other candidates in the 2000 presidential elections include prominent author Li Ao, a former political prisoner who spoke out against the Kuomintang during the White Terror era. Li ran for the New Party, which advocated the status quo and gradual rapprochement with mainland China.

Hsu Hsin-liang, an important figure in Taiwan's underground movement for Taiwan independence and a former political prisoner, ran as an independent after withdrawing from the DPP.

MARCH 11, 2000

Solomon received a telephone call at home from his Uncle Ching Po, a pastor in a Presbyterian church in the Toucheng township of Ilan County and Solomon's only relative in Taiwan.

"Hi, Solomon," said Ching Po.

"Hi, Uncle Ching Po" said Solomon.

"Your grandfather and grandmother are here from the U.S." said Ching Po. "They will be voting during the presidential elections. Do you want to come and meet them?"

The Presbyterian Church in Taiwan had long been known as a driving force for the underground movement for Taiwan independence. Ching Po had once been detained for questioning by the Kuomintang government for his association with political dissidents during his days studying at the seminary.

Solomon knew that his grandparents would vote for Chen Shui-bian and Annette Lu. Despite his resentment against Taiwan independence, Solomon decided to visit his grandparents in Toucheng, a one-and-a-half hour drive from Taipei.

Solomon had lunch with his grandparents at Uncle Ching Po's home before saying goodbye. As an American citizen, Solomon did not have the right to vote in Taiwan.

MARCH 18, 2000

The Central Election Commission completed the tallying of the votes late at night and declared DPP candidates Chen and Lu winners of the 2000 presidential election. Soong came in second with 300,000 less votes, followed by the Kuomintang's Lien and Siew who received some 2 million less votes than Chen and Lu. For the first time in its ninety year history, the Kuomintang was defeated by another political party in the presidential elections.

Analysts blamed Soong's defection from the Kuomintang as a turning point in the KMT presidential campaign, dividing the KMT and losing votes that would have belonged to Lien and Siew.

An empty plaza in the KMT headquarters was all that was left as KMT members and supporters deserted the building following the announcement of Chen and Lu's win. The long-time ruling party which had governed China for over ninety years was stunned and dismayed.

Solomon listened to the radio the night of the election and grew angry as the DPP's Chen and Lu were declared victors. Solomon knew that the DPP and its charter for Taiwan independence was an empty dream, not to mention its strain on relations with mainland China and its effects on instability within the region.

Local radio stations and TV news channels reported thousands of Soong and KMT supporters congregating outside the KMT headquarters near the Chiang Kai-shek Memorial Hall to protest the election results.

At around 10 p.m. after work, Solomon hailed a taxi and headed straight for Chiang Kai-shek Memorial Hall. The road to the KMT headquarters was blocked and Solomon had to walk for fifteen minutes before reaching the Kuomintang building.

As Solomon arrived at the KMT headquarters, he discovered around 100 protesters sitting down outside the entrance to the building. Solomon sat down with the crowd and joined in the chanting "Step down! Lee Teng-hui."

Before long, thousands of people dissatisfied with the election results poured in to Chungshan South Road before the Kuomintang building and blocked the entrance to the presidential residence. Roadblocks were set up from Chunghsiao E. Road in the north to Hsinyi Road to the south as police struggled to contain the demonstrators to a four-mile-long corridor.

Solomon joined the protesters who were moving south to Hsinyi Road and the presidential residence. As the crowd reached the residence, Solomon saw three buses loaded with officials back out from the presidential residence, appearing to escape the protesters.

———

The next day when Solomon came to work, a gloom hung over the reporters and editors in the newsroom. The election win by DPP was not the answer to improving cross-strait relationship nor was it a solution for Taiwan's diplomatic isolation.

Local media did not fail to sensationalize the win by DPP. "The heavens have changed" read a headline in the Chinese language United Daily News.

On the second day after the presidential elections, thousands of protesters continue to fill Chungshan S. Road, demanding the resignation of KMT chairman Lee Teng-hui. Solomon continued to participate in the protests after work.

The third day after the elections, defeated candidate James Soong appeared at the protest at KMT headquarters and requested that the crowds disperse. Meanwhile, police mobilized armored vehicles equipped with water cannons which were used to hit demonstrators outside the presidential residence.

Solomon attended the protests every day after work and on the fifth day, KMT succumbed to the pressure of the masses and forced Lee's resignation. At the same time, Soong bowed to his supporters and announced before the crowds at Chungshan S. Road that he would form a new political party.

A few weeks later, Soong founded the People First Party which gave the people an alternative to the ideologically entrenched Kuomintang and the young, inexperienced DPP.

———

Mainland China continuously called on the ROC to abide by the "One China" principle which states that there is only one China in the world and both the mainland and Taiwan belong in it. This principle was mentioned as part of the 1992 consensus that was reached by Taiwan's Straits Exchange Foundation and the mainland's Association for Relations Across the Taiwan Strait. PRC insisted that the One China principle must be recognized between both sides of the Taiwan Strait for talks to occur.

————

JULY 14, 2000

Constant pressure every day on making the deadline weighs heavily upon any journalist on the job, including Solomon, and the 24-year-old sports editor needed a break from the daily grind. Solomon accumulated enough vacation days to allow him to spend a holiday in Thailand.

With a guidebook in hand, Solomon departed Taiwan on a Swiss Airline flight to Bangkok. Three hours later, Solomon arrived in the Thai capital at 12:00 midnight local time. Passing through immigration with a U.S. passport, Solomon exited the airport and rode the express bus that ran between the airport and downtown Bangkok.

Solomon disembarked from the bus at Bangkok's Chinatown and found a budget hotel which was listed in his guidebook.

The next morning Solomon woke up early at 7 a.m. and boarded the express bus again to Bangkok airport's domestic terminal. Solomon boarded a flight to the island of Ko Samui in southern Thailand. The plane landed at Ko Samui two hours later.

With no bus services between the airport and the beaches, Solomon hired a driver of a pickup truck and arrived at Blue Horizons bungalows situated on a bluff overlooking the ocean on the eastern coast of the island. Solomon chose a bungalow with a view of the ocean. The bungalow operator also provided services including a restaurant and motorcycle rentals.

The green waters off the Ko Samui coastline along with the ocean waves that broke beneath the bungalows gave a healing effect on Solomon. That night, Solomon went to bed early and slept well through the night.

On his second day at Blue Horizons, Solomon rented a motorcycle and began his exploration of the island. Passing through Chaweng Beach, the island's largest stretch of sand which also featured sleazy pole dancers at the beachside bars, Solomon rode on the main road encircling the island and reached Nathon, a harbor at the western end of the island. In the afternoon, Solomon watched the sun set at southern Ko Samui's Jinta Beach with a beer in his hand. On his way back to his bungalow, Solomon stopped at a resort along the main road and ordered coconut chicken for dinner.

Every month during full moon, Ko Samui served as a transit point for the infamous full moon party at the island of Ko Phangan, just a short distance north of Ko Samui. Notorious for use of illegal drugs, the full moon party was the target of occasional police crackdowns.

Solomon missed the full moon party and left Ko Samui after his three day stay. He was the only Asian passenger on board the single engine plane bound for Bangkok.

The connecting flight from Bangkok International Airport to Taipei was delayed for one hour, which allowed Solomon plenty of time to carry his luggage on the long walk from the domestic terminal to the international terminal.

With time to spare, Solomon picked up a book "Jim Thompson: The Unsolved Mystery" at a bookstore in Bangkok Airport, which described the life of a silk tycoon in Thailand who disappeared in the jungle of Malaysia in 1967. Solomon read the book on his flight to Chiang Kai-shek International Airport and at 5:00 p.m., Solomon returned to his desk in the newsroom still with sand in his shoes.

———

SEPTEMBER, 2000

Solomon had worked for The China Courier for two and a half years, more than what he originally planned, and thought about quitting his job soon. The Summer Olympics at Sydney were scheduled to begin on September 15, and Solomon was prepared to resign from his position as sports editor after the Olympics ended.

Two days before the Sydney Games began, the publisher called Solomon into the daily editorial meeting in the conference room. Hsiao asked managing editor Lai to coordinate the newspaper's coverage of the Olympics between Solomon and the page designers. The page designers had selected the Olympic logos and banners from the wire services which Solomon would use in the newspaper's expanded coverage of the Summer Games. Two pages, one black-and-white and one color would be dedicated to the Olympics while another black-and-white page will consist of coverage for other sports.

Solomon came to work earlier than usual to prepare for coverage of the Olympics. As part of the expanded edition of the sports page during the Sydney Olympics, Solomon's duties include editing wire stories, keeping track of medal counts won by Taiwan, editing the Olympics TV schedule, incorporating logos and graphics with the stories on the page, and selecting photographs from the wire services.

Chinese Taipei was expected to medal in the events of women's weight lifting, men's and women's taekwondo, and women's and men's table tennis. Taiwan closed the Olympics with Li Feng-ying and Kuo Yi-hang winning the silver and bronze in women's weightlifting, Huang Chih-hsiung and Chi Shu-ju winning the bronze in men's and women's taekwondo, and Chen Jing winning the bronze in women's table tennis. Chinese Taipei had never won a gold medal in the Olympics and the drought continued at the Sydney Games.

At the closing ceremony, the Australian Olympic committee presented a spectacular fireworks display over the Sydney Harbor Bridge to conclude the memorable 2000 Summer Olympics, and Solomon scanned through the wire services to select the best photos to be used on the sports page.

OCTOBER, 2000

Solomon tendered his resignation letter to the managing editor Paul Lai two days after the curtain fell on the Sydney Olympics. Employees at The China Courier must give a fifteen day advance notice before leaving their positions.

Just one week before Solomon was scheduled to leave his post, publisher Hsiao asked that Solomon list questions that would be used during interviews with future prospective sports editors. Solomon prepared a quiz that tested future editors of their knowledge of the major sporting events around the world and turned it in to Lai.

CHAPTER 11

Solomon remained in Taipei almost half a year after quitting his job. During his two-year stint as a sports editor, Solomon controlled his spending other than an occasional splurge on a pizza or a buffet during his day off. At the time he quit his position, Solomon accumulated some $220,000 New Taiwan Dollars which he kept in his closet after being told by his bank that all savings accounts of foreign currencies would be charged a monthly fee.

Solomon received a phone call from his aunt Victoria in the United States late afternoon in his apartment.

"Hi, Solomon," said Victoria.

"Hi, auntie," said Solomon.

"Are you still working?" said Victoria.

"No," said Solomon.

"How can you survive without working?" said Victoria.

"I have some money saved up," said Solomon.

"I have something to tell you," said Victoria. "Your grandfather has passed away. The funeral will be in two weeks. If you want to come, I will pay for your air ticket,"

"I am planning on moving to another apartment," said Solomon. "I don't think I have the time to return to the U.S."

"O.K." said Victoria

"Bye," said Solomon.

The night after Solomon talked with aunt Victoria though the phone, Solomon left his apartment to buy a drink at a nearby convenience store. After exiting the apartment building and turning into an alleyway, Solomon realized that he had forgotten his wallet. He walked back and reached the door of his apartment. While fumbling for his house key in his pocket, a man dressed in black dashed out from the narrow space between his apartment and the water tower. The man quickly disappeared into the stairway that led to the elevator downstairs.

Solomon entered his apartment and saw the windows of his living room opened. He then quickly checked his closet in the bedroom and found his stash of money gone. Solomon stormed out of the apartment and down the stairs to the elevator. By the time Solomon reached the ground floor, seven minutes had gone by. Solomon ran out of the elevator and charged outside of the apartment only to find nobody around. He then went downstairs to the parking garage at the basement of the apartment building and found no one there.

Months ago, Solomon had taken note of two surveillance cameras that were installed on the alleyway across from his apartment building. Still angry over the loss of his hard-earned money, Solomon knocked on the door of neighborhood chief Chen I-lan who resided just one block away from Solomon's apartment.

"Are you the neighborhood chief?" said Solomon.

"Yes," said Chen.

"My apartment was burglarized last night," said Solomon. "I lost over $200,000 in cash. I noticed that there are surveillance cameras in the alleyway in front of my apartment building. Can I look at the tape?"

"O.K.," said Chen. The neighborhood chief showed Solomon to a computer in the living room of his residence.

"Just enter the date and time when your apartment was burglarized," said Chen.

Solomon soon accessed the surveillance video footage for the time around the burglary of his apartment but still could not find the man in black emerging from the apartment building. "Did you find the burglar?" said Chen.

"No, but thanks for your help," said Solomon.

"You should call the police," said Cheng.

Solomon nodded to the neighborhood chief and left his residence.

Returning to his apartment, Solomon began a visual sweep of his apartment for any clues that the burglar left behind. Solomon discovered a set of footprints leading from the window of his living room to his bedroom closet. He also found fingerprints on a water pipe that extended from the water tower to the wall just outside his living room window.

Solomon placed a call to the Ta-An police station from his home phone.

"This is Ta-An police station," the operator said.

"My apartment was burglarized last night," said Solomon. "I found fingerprints on a wall just outside my living room. Please send someone over."

"We will send a team of officers over," said the operator.

Solomon left his name, phone number, and address to the operator and twenty minutes later two officers knocked on Solomon's door. Solomon opened the door and saw a uniformed officer and a forensics expert.

"Are you Solomon?" asked the uniformed officer.

"Yes," said Solomon.

Solomon led the policemen to the fingerprints on the water pipe outside his living room. The forensics expert carrying a duster examined the fingerprint on the water pipe and shook his head.

"The fingerprints are useless," said the forensics expert. Both policemen then performed a thorough sweep of Solomon's apartment before inquiring of Solomon's background, including his work, finances, and his nationality.

"If you find anything else, give us a call."

———

Noise at Solomon's apartment worsened with the construction of a new lane on the Chien Kuo expressway which ran alongside the apartment building. Solomon tried using earplugs during his sleep but the noise of the heavy equipment overcame his senses. With no more money, Solomon made the decision to move back with his aunt in Los Angeles.

———

JULY 10, 2003

CIA deputy director Adams sent an e-mail to the heads of Directorate of Intelligence, National Clandestine Service, Directorate of Science and Technology, and the Directorate of Support calling for a meeting in the afternoon.

All the Directorate leaders assembled in the conference room of the National Clandestine Service just shortly before Adams walked in to start the meeting.

"Thanks for coming at such short notice," said Adams. "The director and I have decided that there is an urgent need of an in-house china affairs news program to complement our understanding of the mainstream media's China coverage. We have found cases where the American media's coverage of foreign countries outpaced our own information and analysis. For example, national media such as the Washington Post have produced in depth coverage of China's economic development that has proved more timely and accurate than our own sources."

"I am assigning the task of creating our own in-house news program to the Directorate of Support," said Adams. "Emphasis of the coverage should be on the latest developments on foreign countries such as China based on national media and wire services such as the Associated Press, Reuters, and Agence-France Presse. The daily news program, which can be accessed by all levels within the agency, should also contain intelligence from our own sources that are not classified.

I have contacted the National Security Bureau in Taiwan to send a representative familiar with the developments in China to our headquarters and serve as a consultant for our news program.

———

ONE MONTH LATER,

Head of National Security Bureau's operations division Tung Liang landed in Dulles International Airport in Washington D.C. after a fifteen hour flight from Taipei. The exhausted Tung was told that he would be met by someone from the CIA Directorate of Support at the airport. After picking up his baggage, Tung was met by a man holding up a sign with Tung's name.

———

"Mr. Tung Liang?" said Jay Alexander of the CIA Directorate of Support.

"Yes," said Tung.

"Please follow me," said Alexander.

Alexander led Tung out of the airport and continued on to the parking lot where the CIA employee found his Ford Escape. Before long, Alexander and Tung were speeding along the freeway towards Langley, Virginia.

"May I ask what my job here is about?" said Tung.

"You are needed as a consultant for our daily news program," said Alexander. "There is a lot of news coverage on China and we need you for your insider perspective. Our news program will start in one week; so you will have enough time to recuperate from the jet lag."

Alexander and Tung arrived at an apartment complex in Langley two hours after leaving Dulles International Airport.

"We have arranged for an apartment for you to stay," said Alexander. "For now, I will pick you up here every morning at 8 a.m. and we will go to headquarters. Once you receive your salary, you will have the option of buying a car."

———

ONE WEEK LATER,

A man and woman from the Directorate of Support were selected as the anchor for the CIA news program while Tung provided the analysis on the first day of the CIA newscast. The newscast contained news footage by the wire services on significant developments in the United

States, China, and other parts of the world. Unlike the CIA's work on other countries, the agency handled no operatives in China before with the exception of Huang Shan in Hong Kong.

At the end of the newscast, time was allotted for questions for Tung.

"Hu Jintao and Wen Jiabao have been appointed as the president and premier of China" said the male anchor. "Would they pursue democratic reform?"

"Most scholars and analysts from China and Taiwan have voiced their skepticism of the new Chinese leaders pursuing democracy." said Tung.

The female anchor added another question.

"The SARS outbreak in Hong Kong has claimed a large number of victims," said the female anchor. "Is it true that mainland China attempted to censor reports of the outbreak?" "By our analysis, Hong Kong and Taiwan press have given the outbreak full coverage while mainland media have been shunned to publish details of the epidemic," said Tung.

The male anchor followed up with another question.

"Is Taiwan President Chen Shui-bian proposing a "defensive referendum" to try to shape Taiwan's public opinion towards mainland China?" said the male anchor.

"We do not know. But according to the intelligence we acquired, a journalist named Solomon has been the source for a lot of our answers," said Tung.

"Where is this Solomon," asked the female anchor.

"He is working somewhere in the greater China area," said Tung.

CHAPTER 12

Local media in Taiwan had given a "wait-and-see" attitude towards the election win by Chen Shui-bian in 2000. Even newspapers opposed to Taiwan independence such as The China Times and the United Daily News had stated in their commentaries that time would be necessary for President Chen to "adjust to conditions on the road as a new driver." However, three years into Chen's rule the media began to lost patience just as the president proposed a "defensive referendum" to try to steer public opinion in the DPP's favor. Questions which Chen intended to place on the referendum included whether or not Taiwan should purchase more advanced weapons if the mainland launched an attack and whether R.O.C should engage the P.R.C. in negotiations to build peace across the Taiwan Strait.

Chen's push for the referendum came after National Security Bureau intelligence revealed that the mainland had close to five hundred missiles aimed at the island. However, the proposed referendum was deemed irrational and redundant by the local media as well as Taiwan's most important ally, the United States. Despite widespread criticisms, the legislature passed the referendum which was then placed alongside the presidential elections ballot on March 18, 2004.

FEBRUARY, 2004

Campaign for the 2004 presidential elections in Taiwan began with the announcement of a cross-party ticket pairing Kuomintang's former vice president Lien Chan and the People First Party's James Soong. The two would run against incumbent Chen Shui-bian and vice president Annette Lu of the Democratic Progressive Party.

The local media painted the inter-party ticket of Lien Chan and James Soong as a rational alternative to the non-productive government led by President Chen and all polls showed Chen and Lu losing the upcoming presidential elections.

––––––––

MARCH 2004,

One week before the presidential elections, campaigning by the candidates reached a fever pitch. Polls run by local media pointed to a slight advantage by Kuomintang's Lien-Soong pair over the DPP candidates Chen and Lu.

The day before the election, President Chen chose to end his presidential campaign with a sweep of his hometown Tainan on a convoy of open-top jeeps. The move was intended to bolster enough support at Chen's stronghold to lift him and Lu over Lien and Soong.

At 1:45 p.m., Chen was welcomed by Tainan citizens who lighted firecrackers along the way of his convoy. Moments later, Chen felt pain on his stomach and opened his shirt only to find a wound on his abdomen. The president was quickly escorted to a nearby hospital for treatment. A small, open wound on Chen's belly and a bullet hole on the windshield of Chen and Lu's jeep served as evidence that an assassination was carried out by a gunman.

By around 2:30 p.m., the cable news channels were the first to report that the president had been shot during his sweep of Tainan on his open-top jeep, while the three major terrestrial stations all cut in on their regular programming to broadcast the story.

Fortunate that the bullet had only scraped the surface of his abdomen, Chen escaped the assassination attempt receiving only stitches. The hospital discharged Chen in the evening with Chen walking out under his own power.

———

After Chen's assassination attempt, Lien publicly stated that he would defer to the Central Election Commission as to whether or not the presidential election should still be held the next day.

Late evening, the Central Election Commission announced that the presidential election will continue as scheduled despite the attempted assassination on Chen.

The story of Chen's attempted assassination dominated the news and the talk shows on the eve of the election with many analysts predicting that Chen might earn enough sympathy votes to sway the electorate in his favor.

On March 18, the results of the presidential election were released late in the evening with DPP's Chen and Lu notching a narrow victory over the inter-party pair of Lien and Soong. Chen and Lu won the election by around 3,000 votes or .22 percent of the total votes over second place Lien and Soong. Unable to accept the outcome, Lien and

Soong vowed to file lawsuits to nullify the election results. Lien and Soong argued that the assassination attempt on Chen had unfairly swung the election in Chen and Lu's favor.

As for the defensive referendum that was placed alongside the presidential elections ballot, the number of votes on the referendum did not exceed the minimum needed for it to take effect. The defensive referendum was thus declared invalid.

Solomon became glued to the Chinese language channels in Los Angeles providing live feed of the election results from Taiwan. Disappointed with Chen and Lu's win, Solomon still planned on returning to work at The China Courier.

———

Mainland China's engagement with the Republic of China continued as top mainland officials openly extended their invitation to members of the Democratic Progressive Party in Taiwan to visit the mainland on the condition that they accept the One China principle.

CHAPTER 13

OCTOBER 29, 2006

Five years since moving back to Los Angeles from Taiwan, Solomon saved enough money to return to work at The China Courier when Solomon's aunt Victoria suggested that they take a vacation in Germany before he leaves.

Both agreed that the two visited Germany as part of a group tour. Solomon picked up a brochure of a European tour operator at a travel agency near his home. Aunt Victoria perused the list of tours on Germany and decided to take the 14-day circle tour.

The earliest of the available Germany circle tour tours came in November and Aunt Victoria paid the bill in full two weeks before the trip was scheduled to start. Solomon held high expectations for what would be his third trip to Europe, yet little did he know a turbulent ordeal would befall him in Germany.

Winnie Lam was packing her clothes for her flight tomorrow to Germany where she will pursue her MBA. After she graduated from UCLA, she took on a job as an account executive for AT&T and handled the corporate accounts out of the Los Angeles office. Nine years into her job, a climb into management required a business degree. She applied to the University of Heidelberg business school because she longed to study and live in Europe.

NOVEMBER 14, 2006

Solomon and Aunt Victoria landed in Frankfurt in the morning and found the hotel shuttle outside the airport with little difficulty.

Ten minutes later, Solomon and Aunt Victoria were speeding towards the Holiday Inn in Frankfurt. With much experience in traveling, Solomon had packed light, bringing along only a rolling duffle bag and a backpack.

Aunt Victoria had arranged to arrive in Frankfurt two days before the group tour started so she and Solomon can have time to become familiar with the city. The two checked in at the hotel with a middle-aged Asian couple behind them in line. Aunt Victoria asked the couple if they were on the Germany tour.

"Are you on the Globus tour?" said Aunt Victoria.

"Yes, are you?" said the woman.

"Yeah, we came two days ahead so we can see Frankfurt," said Aunt Victoria.

"I'll see you later," said the woman before she and her husband took their turn checking in.

Aunt Victoria and Solomon rode the taxi to the Frankfurt Opera House in old town Alstadt. The two then walked about twenty minutes southeast and came upon Romerburg, an open plaza surrounded by half-timbered houses in the heart of Frankfurt. A short distance south of

Romerburg lies the River Main where Solomon and Aunt Victoria embarked on a short cruise and sailed through the heart of Frankfurt.

The second day of their stay in Frankfurt, Aunt Victoria and Solomon boarded the subway to Palmengarten, Frankfurt's only arboretum, just a few kilometers north of the Alstadt. The garden displayed plants from all continents and featured a glass dome which provided climate control for exotic plants, including a handful of twenty-foot palm trees native to the tropics.

Outside the glass dome, a photography exhibit of plant life impressed Solomon with the sharpness of its images. Solomon remembered what his father, an award-winning amateur photographer in Taiwan said, that German camera lenses were the best in the world.

———

On day one of the Globus Germany circle tour, Solomon, Aunt Victoria, and the rest of the tour members set off from the hotel in Frankfurt and by noon reached a village where the group would take a cruise along the Rhine.

Three hours later, tour members disembarked the river boat and boarded the tour bus heading for the city of Cologne where they stopped alongside the majestic Cologne Cathedral, one of the few churches in Germany spared by Allied bombing during World War II.

Solomon spent half an hour browsing the gothic cathedral's interior before climbing twenty minutes to the top of one of the cathedral's two spires for a view of the entire city of Cologne.

The next day, the tour brought the group to Hamburg,

Germany's largest port city where a two-day stop was scheduled on the itinerary.

In the early evening, Armando drove the tour members from their hotel at the outskirts of Hamburg to a restaurant which served authentic local cuisine in the city. The restaurant treated each of their guests to a tender steak which won good reviews from the tour members. Situated along the Elbe River which meets the North Sea to the north, Hamburg is notorious for its red light district Reeperbahn. On the tour bus, the group was given a quick peek of the young prostitutes along the street before being whisked away to their hotel.

The next day, Solomon and Aunt Victoria opted to pay extra to take the excursion to Lubeck, a town located a short distance away from Hamburg. Armando, the driver, picked up those who had chosen the excursion at the Hamburg seaport at noon and drove off for Lubeck, a commercial center during medieval times.

A local guide met the group in Lubeck and led the way on foot for what would become an hour-long walking tour through northern Germany's center of trade during the medieval age. Towards the end of the tour, the tour members were taken inside the Marienkirche, a church in Lubeck's old town Altstadt. While the group sat on the pews listening to the local guide's introduction of Lubeck, a military helicopter flew low over the church and produced a loud roar that broke the attention of the group, including Solomon. The noise shook Solomon, who took fifteen minutes to breath at a normal rhythm again. This was a recurring condition which Solomon experiences every time he goes to Europe.

Twenty minutes later, the walking tour ended at a chocolate shop south of the Marienkirche.

As Armando drove the group from Lubeck back to the

hotel, the local guide delivered the bad news. Tour guide Kral had succumbed to illness, the type of which was not revealed, and a new tour guide would be taking over.

Later in the evening during dinner, Paul Schumann of Austria introduced himself as the new tour guide and shook hands with everyone on the tour group table to table. Before going to bed that night, Solomon drank a bottle of complimentary German beer kept cold inside the room's refrigerator before falling asleep.

The next day, Schumann appeared to be as competent and knowledgeable as Kral while the tour group pressed ahead on the autobahn past the electricity-generating wind turbines along the way east towards Berlin.

After arriving in the German capital, the group stopped for three days touring the sights of the city including the last remaining sections of the Berlin Wall, the Brandenburg Gate, and Kaiser-Wilhelm Dom, a damaged church lying in the modern, bustling shopping district of former West Berlin. The group also visited Checkpoint Charlie, the guard post which stood as a poignant reminder of the Berliners' divisive past during World War II, and the Berlin suburb of Potsdam where Winston Churchill, Harry Truman, and Joseph Stalin met in the Potsdam Conference after the Nazi surrender in 1945.

Two days after leaving Berlin, Solomon, Aunt Victoria and the rest of the tour members arrived in Dresden, a former East German town. Rebuilt since the Allied bombing of World War II, Dresden boasts cultural jewels such as the Frauenkirche, a church restored to its former splendor in 2005, the Zwinger museums, and the Residenzschloss, the former royal palace which houses the Green Vaults: a collection of jewelry and porcelain available to view by the public.

That evening, dinner was served at the ballroom of

Novotel Dresden where the tour group was staying in. At the end of the dinner, a group member with family ties to the Czech Republic, Mary Gandalovic, stood up and called the group to attention.

"Everybody, I have news to report about our former tour guide Sasha Kral. She has told me over the telephone that she had fallen ill and hopes to soon recuperate." said Gandalovic. "Sasha also told us not to worry over her condition and continue to enjoy the remainder of the tour."

Just as Gandolovic concluded her announcement, a female member of the tour, Rose Taylor, was overcome with a seizure at the dining table. Taylor was shaking uncontrollably when aunt Victoria, a former nurse in Hong Kong, rushed to her side and held her arms tight. The seizure persisted for another five minutes and Schumann called the paramedics. Fifteen minutes later, Dresden paramedics arrived at the hotel ball room and placed an oxygen mask over Taylor, who soon improved to the point where she can breathe normally again.

Unexpected interludes continue to dog Solomon and Aunt Victoria's tour when the group was leaving Nurenburg on the ninth day of their Germany circle tour.

The hard-working Schumann had just finished leading a walking tour to the central market square Hauptmarkt and signaled for Armando to depart for Munich. As Armando was heading for the autobahn, the driver of a silver Mercedes parked along the curb opened his door and hit the right side of the Globus bus as it passed by.

Armando stopped and stepped out of the bus along with Schumann to examine the damage on the bus: a one-meter long dent on the bus' right side. Schumann called the police from his cell phone and twenty minutes later two policemen came to the scene of the traffic accident. Armando wrote down the I.D. and the personal information of the driver. After a forty-minute delay, the bus tour continued on its way to Munich.

That night after arriving in their hotel in Munich, tour members visited the traditional German beer house Hofbrauhas where the group drank a stein of beer and danced to live Bavarian music.

The tour group boarded the bus at 7:45 a.m. from their hotel in Munich on the tenth day of the Germany circle tour with the town square Marienplatz as their next destination. Schumann scheduled two hours for the group to stroll through Munich's old town Alstadt and watch the Glockenspiel; automatic figurines moving to the chime of bells and telling stories of the royalty atop New City Hall at Marienplatz.

From Munich, Solomon, Aunt Victoria, and the rest of the tour group proceeded to the foot of Castle Neuschwanstein in the Bavarian countryside. The inspiration for Walt Disney's Disneyland castle was built by King Ludwig II in the nineteenth century.

Cruising on the way from the Black Forest towards Heidelberg on the autobahn, the tour bus was pulled over by the German Polizei.

"May I see your driver's license and transportation documents?" the Polizei officer said.

"Sure," said Armando.

"Where did your bus come from before you reached Germany?"

"I finished a tour in Switzerland and drove here for the Globus Germany tour,"

The Polizei officer read the documents and reached for his radio. After reporting to command central, he turned and faced Armando.

"We need to detain this bus before we can confirm your vehicle license," said the officer.

Schumann immediately stepped in and protested.

"But officer, we have an itinerary to keep," said Schumann.

"This is the law," said the officer before he called in on his radio to request for more patrol cars.

Thirty minutes, later four patrol cars were escorting the Globus bus to a small town in the Black Forest. The tour group was given mineral water while they waited inside the police station. Two hours later, the police gave Armando permission to continue on his trip.

"Fortunately, Armando has produced all the necessary papers," Schumann said through the bus microphone as the tour group moved on to Stuttgart. "I have never seen so much trouble in all the tours that I have worked on."

On the last day of the fourteen-day trip, the group came to the picturesque university town of Heidelberg for the final stop before returning to Frankfurt. Solomon and Aunt Victoria spent the early morning walking through Heidelberg University, the old town, and Heidelberg Castle, which provides a panoramic view of the town below and the River Neckar.

Solomon asked to be separated from Aunt Victoria so he can have more time to walk the town by himself. As he began to cross the bridge over River Neckar, Solomon recognized a familiar figure standing at the middle of the bridge. As he walked closer, he made out the face of the Asian woman to be Winnie.

"Hi Winnie," said Solomon.

Winnie took a look at Solomon. Taken by surprise, she hid her emotions and gave a polite smile.

"Hi Solomon, what are you doing here?"

"I'm with a tour, with my aunt," said Solomon.

"Where were you all these years?" said Winnie.

"I was in Taiwan working as a journalist," said Solomon.

The two looked across the river towards Heidelberg University under the afternoon sun and shared a moment together. Solomon smiled. Winnie smiled too.

CHAPTER 14

NOVEMBER 28, 2006

The China Airlines flight CI005 carrying Solomon landed at Chiang Kai-shek International Airport at 9 p.m. local time, the first time that he stepped foot on Taiwan in five years.

Solomon cleared customs and immigration using his U.S. passport and proceeded to the airport's public transportation waiting area where he boarded a bus for Taipei with hopes of returning to work at The China Courier.

At 10:00 p.m., Solomon stepped off the bus at Miramar Hotel and checked-in for two nights as he prepared to search for an apartment in the city.

Solomon browsed the classified ads of China Times the next day and found a studio located just a ten-minute walk from The China Courier building. The small studio was fully furnished complete with a large screen television, a refrigerator, DSL internet, and hardwood floors.

DECEMBER 1, 2006

Solomon called The China Courier operator from his cell phone and requested to speak with managing editor Paul Lai.

"Hello, Mr. Lai. I'm Solomon. Do you remember me?" Solomon said.

"Yes," said Lai.

"I'm in Taipei right now. I want to come back and work at the National Desk," said Solomon.

"I will have to talk to the publisher about that," said Lai. "I will call you later. What is your phone number?"

Solomon gave Lai his cell phone number and hung up.

Two hours later, Solomon received a call from Lai.

"Hi, Solomon," said Lai. "The publisher wants to meet with you tomorrow at the newsroom at 4 p.m." said Lai.

"O.K." said Solomon.

"Then I'll see you tomorrow," said Lai before hanging up.

The next day at the scheduled time, Solomon walked through the front door of The China Courier where a security guard stood.

"What is your business here?" said the security guard.

"I have an appointment with the publisher," said Solomon.

"What is your name?" said the guard.

"Solomon."

The security guard flipped through the pages of his daily log and found Solomon's name.

"Please sign here on the log," said the guard.

Solomon signed his name and then entered the elevator. The former employee exited the elevator on the fifth floor and saw managing editor Lai sitting at his desk in the newsroom just as like it was before.

"Hi, Mr. Lai," said Solomon.

"Hi," said Lai. "Please come with me to the conference room."

The former co-workers walked into the conference room which also contained a library of the newspaper's clippings from the past.

"The publisher will meet with you soon," said Lai before leaving Solomon alone in the room. Solomon picked up the file on cross-strait affairs and read for almost one hour when the publisher appeared.

Both sat down across the conference table as Hsiao held a file of Solomon's past clips in his hands.

"The managing editor told me that you want to work at the National Desk," said Hsiao.

"Yes," said Solomon.

"What particular subject are you interested in?" said Hsiao.

"Cross-strait affairs," said Solomon.

"Since you don't have experience at the national desk, I am assigning you to the position of a translator before you can go out into the field," said Hsiao.

"O.K." said Solomon.

―――――

JANUARY 22, 2007

After two months of translating news articles from the United Evening News and Central News Agency wire service, Solomon was assigned the cross-strait affairs and defense beats.

National desk editor John Fu handed Solomon his first

assignment on the national desk: the Ministry of Defense's (MND) reaction to the PRC's test fire of a long range missile into the Pacific Ocean. The results of the long range missile test fire had been released by mainland China's defense ministry to the Chinese and international press and received wide coverage. The MND was scheduled to hold a news conference the next day detailing Taiwan's response to the test fire.

The next day, Solomon woke up early and took the bus to the Taipei Train Station where he walked approximately one kilometer past the Presidential Office to the adjacent MND building. At 10 a.m. sharp, MND spokesman Major Oong Chung-yi opened the press conference.

"Thank you for attending today's press briefing. As all of you may know, the mainland has successfully test fired a long range missile into the Pacific Ocean capable of reaching our nation. We strongly oppose any form of provocation by the mainland's side. The military has made all preparations necessary to meet the threat posed by the mainland's long range missiles," said Oong.

Oong's statement drew jeers by a handful of reporters on the front rows who had expected that the MND would announce its position on the arms purchase bill which had been stalled in the Legislature. Nevertheless, the press conference continued with Oong answering questions on the arms procurement bill as well as the PRC missile test fire. After the press briefing ended, Solomon approached Major Oong and introduced himself as a reporter for The China Courier while the two exchanged name cards.

"Hello, Major," said Solomon.

"Nihao, Mr. Solomon," said Oong after reading the reporter's title on the name card.

"I think I am the only English press here today," said Solomon.

"You are right," said Oong.

"Do you have anything for me that I can use besides the MND reaction?" said Solomon.

"I'm not supposed to give this to the press corps yet but I'll make an exception for you as we need to make our position clear to the international community," said Oong.

The major reached for his briefcase and pulled out a press release before handing it over to Solomon.

The MND press release read:

"TAIPEI, TAIWAN – Mainland China has successfully test fired a long range missile into the Pacific Ocean which gives the PRC the ability to strike U.S. military bases as far as Guam in a potential attack on Taiwan.

Meanwhile, the number of mainland China ballistic and cruise missiles aimed at Taiwan have increased to more than 800.

In addition, according to the latest intelligence obtained by the MND, mainland China's newly developed Jian-10 fighter jets have been deployed in airbases in southern China within striking range of the R.O.C.

The Jian-10 fighter possesses functions similar to that of Taiwan's F-16A/Bs jets and together with the mainland's Russian-made Su-27 and Su-30 fighter jets can command air superiority over Taiwan.

We continue to urge the Legislature's passage of the arms procurement bill which includes the purchase of Patriot missile systems, submarines, and anti-submarine aircraft from the United States."

Solomon filed the story with National Desk editor Fu, leading with the Jian-10 fighters and the intelligence contained in the MND press release.

———

National desk editor John Fu and managing editor Paul Lai were the only China Courier employees remaining since Solomon returned after quitting his position in 2000. Solomon worked alongside Erika Ting as the only two reporters at the National desk. International page editor Yi Kui-chu handled the editing of the sports page.

The economic downturn that the U.S. media experienced for most of the first decade of the twentieth first century also impacted Taiwan. Several Chinese-language newspapers including the lifestyle-oriented Minsheng Pao, the China Times Evening News, and the state-run Central Daily have shut down.

Instead, the readership in Taiwan has been force fed tabloids such as the Apple Daily and the Next weekly, subsidiaries of Hong Kong's Next media which places emphasis of its coverage on celebrity gossip and sensational reporting.

———

FEBRUARY 14, 2007

The biggest news since the re-election of Chen Shuibian in 2004 rocked Taiwan politics and Taiwan society when Kuomintang star and former Taipei mayor Ma Yingjeou was indicted for corruption.

Kuomintang chairman Ma had earned an image in Taiwan as "Mr. Clean" during the course of his political career from Mainland Affairs Council spokesman to Minister of Justice and finally as Taipei mayor.

Much speculation had surrounded Ma over his intent to run for the presidency in 2008 after stepping down as Taipei mayor in 2006.

On the same day the corruption charges were laid out against Ma by prosecutors; Ma announced that he would resign as Kuomintang chairman and launch his presidential campaign for the 2008 elections.

Prosecutors charged that Ma embezzled NT$11 million from a special expense account during his tenure as Taipei mayor.

Solomon first saw Ma's indictment on the local cable news channel and came to work in the newsroom as usual early evening. The clatter of the computer keyboard filled the entire newsroom as the China Courier journalists weighed in on the repercussions of Ma's indictment.

"What will happen next?" managing editor Paul Lai asked Solomon as he sifted through the day's press releases besides Lai's desk.

"I think he would still run for the president as an independent," said Solomon.

Solomon was told by National desk editor John Fu to wait for any follow ups coming through the Chinese wire service on the breaking story that would needed to be rewritten from Chinese to English.

Towards the 10:30 p.m. deadline for the National Desk, Solomon was given a short piece to write on KMT's cancellation of its year-end banquet in the wake of Ma's indictment.

MARCH 4, 2007

Intending to make his mark on history, President Chen Shui-bian had presented his view of the Taiwan-mainland China relationship in a speech widely known as the "Four Wants and One Without" statement that had drew wide criticism from the United States and mainland China. In the speech, Chen had said "Taiwan wanted independence, name rectification, a new constitution, and economic development without the left or right of the road issue."

The statement drew strong reaction from mainland China, which had said that anyone trying to split Taiwan from China was a "sinner of history." The United States reiterated the U.S. position of not supporting Taiwan independence.

MARCH 10, 2007

The weekly press conference for the top Cabinet advisory body for the cross-strait relationship Mainland Affairs Council was scheduled to be held at 5 p.m. in the Ministry of Foreign Affairs Building on Chungshan South Road. Told by National desk editor Fu to ask a question on the Four Wants and One Without speech, Solomon arrived at the MAC press conference room five minutes early and found a seat in the front row.

It was MAC Vice Chairman Pan Meng-de, as always, who showed up for the press conference and who immediately began his statement after greeting the reporters.

"The Mainland Affairs Council puts stability across the Taiwan Strait as its number one goal and will continue to oversee negotiations on allowing mainland tour groups to visit the R.O.C., " Pan said.

"Any questions?" asked Pan.

Solomon raised his hand immediately and earned the first question.

"Has negotiations on the mainland tour group been affected by President Chen Shui-bian's speech?" asked Solomon.

"The Mainland Affairs Council will continue steps to promote cross-strait exchanges and will oversee negotiations on allowing mainland tour groups to Taiwan in the shortest time possible as part of the government's policy to engage with mainland China," said Pan before taking a slight bow and leaving the room.

Solomon filed his story one hour later with National Desk editor Fu leading with how the Mainland Affairs Council downplayed President Chen's Four Wants and One Without speech.

MARCH 17, 2007

Solomon arrived at the Westin Taipei ball room at twelve noon having been assigned by the National Desk editor Fu to cover the European Chamber of Commerce Taipei's monthly luncheon.

"The ECCT is expected to make an important announcement," Fu had said.

Solomon was greeted by the ECCT press officer outside the ballroom and led to the table where a handful of Chinese language reporters sat. After a three-course lunch, the ECCT press officer handed a folder to each reporter at the table titled "2007 ECCT Position Papers."

"The chairman will go over details of this year's position papers," the ECCT press officer said.

Five minutes later, ECCT chairman Matthew Wendt stepped onto the podium.

"We have released this year's position papers," Wendt said. "I would like to review some important points contained in this year's papers."

"First of all, we call on the government to speed up normalizing relations with mainland China," said Wendt. "Taiwan must break out of its isolation by normalizing relations with the People's Republic of China."

"We commend the ongoing talks between Taiwan and mainland travel organizations on allowing mainland tour groups into Taiwan. The ECCT also calls for unrestricted direct transportation, postal, and commercial links with mainland China, or the Three Links, which is crucial to lifting Taiwan's slumping economy," said Wendt.

Solomon filed the story leading with Wendt's call for improved relations with the mainland.

———

MARCH 25, 2006

One week before Ma Ying-jeou's trial was scheduled to begin, Solomon logged on to the Taipei District Court website to enter a lottery for the distribution of press passes to journalists covering the trial. The trial was not open to members of the public although a large contingent of domestic and foreign media outlets was expected to attend the trial.

Two days later, Solomon logged on to the Taipei District Court website and found that he had been assigned a press pass to Ma's corruption trial.

The following Monday morning, Solomon rode the Mass Rapid Transit subway line two blocks from his apartment to Chiang Kai-shek Memorial Hall station and walked one kilometer to the Taipei District Court.

Inside the courthouse, Solomon presented his press I.D. to a clerk at the administration office and received his press pass. Fifteen minutes before the trial began, Solomon climbed the stairs to the second floor and found a crowd of reporters lining up for security check outside a courtroom.

Solomon joined the line and ten minutes later entered the courtroom where he took a seat along with approximately twenty other journalists.

Right before the trial began, DPP legislator Lin Chong-mou created a commotion outside the courtroom repeatedly yelling "Unfair justice" as he was denied access to the trial by police. Lin's rant continued when Ma and his attorney was entering the courtroom. The ruckus outside did not seem to rattle Ma as the seasoned politician sat down behind the defendant's table and prepared his case. Before long, the court was brought to order with the judge's entrance and the door was closed, bringing peace back in the courtroom.

At the opening of the trial, Judge Tsai Shou-shun read the charges out loud and asked Ma how he would plea.

"I am not guilty of the corruption charges and have never committed any crimes of corruption," declared Ma.

Ma was indicted with transferring some NT$11 million from a special expense account to his private bank account during his tenure as Taipei mayor between 1998 and 2006.

In the middle of the trial, the judge called for an half-hour break from the proceedings and all the reporters were ordered to leave the courtroom. Solomon noticed former China Courier copy editor Peter Manning during the trial and saw him again outside the courtroom.

"Hi, Peter," said Solomon.

"Hi, Solomon," said Manning.

"Not guilty, Ma declares," said Manning.

"Yes," said Solomon. "Who do you work for now?"

"I'm with Reuters," said Manning. "And you?"

"I'm still at The China Courier," said Solomon.

"Is Paul Lai still there?" asked Manning.

"Yes," said Solomon.

———

During the trial, Ma defended himself by citing four cases in which the special expense account in question was determined to be as part of the official's salary and that those cases should serve as precedents in the judge's deliberation.

"I believe that the use of the special expense account should be at the official's own discretion and that the charges brought against me are flawed," Ma said during the trial.

At the end of the trial's opening day, a box containing receipts which prosecutors charged Ma had used to claim the special expense account was handed over to the Judge Tsai.

Solomon filed the story with National Desk editor Fu, leading with Ma's not-guilty declaration.

CHAPTER 15

The Ministry of National Defense press conference was scheduled to be held at 8 a.m. in the morning and Solomon arrived as usual five minutes early. A press release detailing the ongoing Han Kuang military exercise was being passed through the scores of reporters present as the MND spokesman Luo Mu-di entered the room and began his statement.

"The two-month-long Han Kuang military exercise is reaching its final weeks and we are pleased to say that the drills have gone smoothly," said Luo. "Our computer simulation of the battle scenarios which have been executed all pointed to a successful defense of a mainland attack."

"As for the PAC-3 Patriot missiles that have drawn wide attention from the public, we are pleased to announce that the tests yielded four hits out of seven which falls within the normal parameters of a Patriot missile system," said Luo.

Much to the surprise of Solomon, the press release in his hand contained a map of the PAC-3 missile systems which were being deployed on the island. The Patriot missiles, which have seen action in the Gulf War intercepting SCUD missiles, were installed in Taiwan for the purpose of intercepting mainland China missiles in an event of an attack on the island.

"To better inform the public, we have included a map of the PAC-3 deployments on the island in the press release," said Luo.

"Are there any questions?" asked Luo.

"A long silence fell over the press conference room.

"Moving on to the next topic, we are introducing a new tactical missile system that has been designed to respond to a mainland missile attack," said Luo.

"The Tactical Shorebase Missile For Fire Suppression has been deployed on the outer islands and will react to a mainland missile attack by striking mainland China's airports and missile batteries.

"TSMFS is a passive weapons system that will only target the mainland's military installations," said Luo. "Our intelligence has revealed that mainland China has positioned over 800 cruise missiles aimed at Taiwan."

"In conclusion, despite the overall success of the Han Kuang military exercise, the drills showed weaknesses in parts of our defense that urgently calls for the passage of the arms procurement bill that is being stalled in the legislature," said Luo.

"We urge legislators to quickly pass the arms procurement bill," said Luo before taking a bow and leaving the room.

Solomon filed the story with National Desk editor Fu, leading with the TSMFS.

MAY 1, 2007

CIA chief of Intelligence and Analysis Robert Grier was reading the daily press clippings prepared by the Office of Asian Pacific Analysis when he noticed a China Courier article written by Solomon on Taiwan's tactical missile system. Grier remembered the name Solomon which was mentioned in the in-house news program numerous times by Tung Liang as a source for Taiwan's National Security Bureau.

Grier quickly placed a call to deputy director Adams.

"This is Adams,

"This is Grier from intelligence and analysis."

"I found Solomon. He is a reporter for a Taiwan newspaper The China Courier. I have his press clipping," said Grier.

"Bring me the press clipping," said Adams before hanging up.

Twenty minutes later Grier appeared at Adam's door and placed the press clipping on Adam's desk.

"Is this the only article you have by Solomon?" asked Adams.

"Yes," said Grier.

"I want to know every article that he has written," said Adams.

"Yes, sir," said Grier before stepping out of the office.

Adams read Solomon's article on Taiwan's tactical missile system and searched online for The China Courier website in Taiwan. The deputy director located the newspaper website and wrote down the address of The China Courier building before placing a call to the head of Office of Asian Pacific Analysis Casey Coffey.

"This is Couffey,"

"This is Deputy Director Adams. I need you to contact Tung Liang of Taiwan's National Security Bureau and request any information on a newspaper reporter for The China Courier named Solomon," Adams said.

"Yes, sir," said Couffey.

———

MAY 9, 2007

The day's breaking news was the crash of a F-5F fighter jet during the annual Han Kuang exercise which killed two Taiwan pilots as well as two Singaporean soldier on the ground.

By early afternoon, Solomon placed a call to his press contact at the Ministry of National Defense Major Pai Chiang.

"Major Pai, this is The China Courier's Solomon,"

"Nihao, Solomon." said Major Pai.

"Can you give me the details of the jet crash," said Solomon.

"Everything that needs to be said on the jet crash was covered by MND minister Lee Jye at the press conference at noon," said Major Pai.

"Do you have a press release on the jet crash?" said Solomon.

"We have not issued a press release yet," said Major Pai.

"The evening news and CNA have reported that there are two Singaporean fatalities," said Solomon.

"I will not comment on that," said Major Pai.

Solomon hung up and decided to wait for further details that might emerge.

At 4 p.m., Solomon received a fax from the Singapore Ministry for Defence stating that two Singapore soldiers were injured from the jet crash and were being treated at the hospital while seven others received minor injuries.

Solomon placed a call to Major Pai.

"Hi, Major Pai," said Solomon. "I have received a press release from the Singapore Ministry for Defence which stated nine Singaporean soldiers were injured. Can you confirm that?"

"I cannot confirm that," said Major Pai. "If you can, please leave that part out of your story."

"Both the United Evening News and the Central News Agency have reported two Singapore fatalities from the jet crash," said Solomon. "I must include that in my story."

After Solomon hung up, a press release from the Air Force Command Headquarters came through the newsroom's fax machine. The press release contained a brief, two-paragraph statement mentioning the jet crash and the deaths of the two pilots and two others on the ground.

The only explanation that came to Solomon for the MND's lack of reaction to the crash was the military's fear of turning the incident into an international affair which could draw a reaction from mainland China.

Solomon told the National desk editor Fu on the military's wish to keep the jet crash from escalating into an international incident.

"The military doesn't want to draw a reaction from mainland China," said Solomon.

"Keep the deaths of the Singaporean soldiers in the story but off the lead," said Fu.

———

MAY 14, 2007

National desk editor Fu received an e-mail from the Taiwan Endemic Species Research Institute (TESRI) which stated that a strip of endangered moss near the western coast was being threatened by Chinese Petroleum Corporation digging.

Two photos of the strip of moss were attached to the e-mail, which also commended The China Courier's recent coverage of conservation efforts by Taiwan's environmental organizations.

Fu decided to give the story to Solomon and forwarded the TESRI statement to Solomon's e-mail.

"Check your in-box," Fu said to Solomon in the newsroom. "I have given you a story."

After reading over the TESRI statement, Solomon called the number on the e-mail and reached TESRI assistant researcher Tseng Chin-yu.

"Hello, Mr. Tseng. This is Solomon from The China Courier. I received your fax," said Solomon.

"Hello, Solomon," said Tseng.

"Did you write the e-mail?" said Solomon.

"Yes," Tseng said.

"When were the photos taken?" said Solomon.

"We took those photos two weeks ago," said Tseng.

"Have you sent your e-mail to other news media?" said Solomon.

"No," said Tseng. "I sent the e-mail only to your newspaper because of your recent coverage on Taiwan's conservation efforts."

"Thank you," said Solomon. "I will call you if I have any more questions on the story."

Realizing that he had an exclusive story on his hands, Solomon finished writing the story just minutes before the deadline.

AUGUST 14, 2007

The four-month long corruption trial of former Taipei mayor Ma Ying-jeou ended with his acquittal by the Taipei District Court. The judge cleared Ma of all charges of corruption and breach of trust on the grounds that he never intended to embezzle a special expense account during his tenure as Taipei mayor.

"I call for the revamping of existing rules to better protect basic human rights, so that no one will fall victim to the unnecessary legal hassles as I have," said Ma at a news conference after the verdict.

SEPTEMBER 5, 2007

Solomon arrived at work late afternoon and found a wire print-out on his desk with the headline "Mainland Affairs Council approves Yao Ming visit," by Agence France-presse. The story that followed detailed how both the ROC and PRC authorities have reached an agreement to allow the NBA star to come to Taiwan.

Solomon placed a call to the Chinese Taipei Basketball Association and reached the director general Lang Yung-yung.

"This is director general Lang,"

"Mr. Lang, this is Solomon from The China Courier. Is Yao Ming coming to Taiwan?"

"Yes," said Lang. "I just got off the phone with the PRC basketball association. They have approved Yao's visit next week."

"Do you have the itinerary of his visit?" said Solomon.

"No, I will send it to you once it is set," said Lang.

TWO DAYS LATER,

Solomon picked up Yao Ming's itinerary that was faxed to The China Courier newsroom which indicated that he will participate in a charity event at the Hsinchu Science Park benefiting aboriginal children and play in a charity basketball game the following day between a team of Taiwan celebrities and the Taiwan professional league all stars.

SEPTEMBER 9, 2007

Solomon took the one-hour bus ride from Taipei to Hsinchu then hailed a cab headed straight for the Hsinchu Science Park, home to Taiwan's tech giants and the island nation's Silicon Valley. The cabbie dropped him off at the Hsinchu Science Park gymnasium where a crowd gathered outside.

Solomon showed his press I.D. to the security at the door and passed through with no trouble. The seasoned reporter estimated a crowd of around three hundred waiting inside the gym. Solomon was half an hour early and well-prepared for his job this day. The night before, he had researched Yao on the internet and found out that he had just been married to a PRC women's basketball team member and that he had returned from his honeymoon to play for the PRC men's basketball team.

At exactly 2 p.m., Yao entered the Hsinchu Science Park gymnasium to the roar of the crowd's cheer as the M.C. announced his arrival. Mainland China's Yao then mingled with aboriginal children and played a game of three-on-three with the disadvantaged kids.

For the purpose of "cross-strait basketball exchange" as dubbed by the organizers, Yao participated in a question and answer session with the children and shared parts of personal life.

Solomon filed the story with National Desk editor Fu, leading with Yao's interaction with aboriginal children in the charity event.

———

THE NEXT DAY,

Solomon boarded a city bus for the National Taiwan University gymnasium at eight in the morning and arrived twenty minutes later. He entered and found a seat along press row. Solomon was disappointed to find a crowd of only a few hundred at hand in the gymnasium to witness the NBA star in action.

The game pitted Yao and a team of celebrities against an all-star squad from Taiwan's professional basketball league. In a half-hearted affair by both sides, the game ended with Yao's team taking the loss.

———

No official statistics of the game were kept as the organizers attempted to play down the winners and losers of the cross-strait match. Furthermore, Yao was not allowed to give interviews after the game. Solomon tried to ambush Yao's entourage for a question as the NBA star was leaving the gymnasium only to be pushed back by security.

Solomon filed the story with National Desk editor Fu, leading with Yao's performance during the game.

SEPTEMBER 25, 2007

On his day off from work, Solomon visited the Taipei Central Library across from the Ta An Park to read foreign newspapers and magazines not available at the local branch libraries.

Solomon picked up a copy of the latest Time magazine at the periodicals section and sat down at a reading table. After perusing through the magazine, Solomon recognized the private investigator whom he had hired in 1999 sitting at a reading table across from Solomon.

He put down the newspaper which he was reading and approached Solomon.

"Hello," he said.

"Hi," said Solomon.

"I have some friends who work at the National Security Bureau." He said. "I can make your problem go away for $40,000 New Taiwan Dollars."

"How did you know that I'm here?" asked Solomon.

"I followed you from your apartment," said the private investigator. "It is not hard for P.I.s to find out where someone lives."

"I don't want any more help," said Solomon before standing up and walking away.

———

SEPTEMBER 30, 2007

Coming to work as usual at 4 p.m., Solomon told managing editor Lai that he intended to quit and turned in his resignation letter to the twenty-year China Courier employee. Completing his last day of work two weeks later, Solomon said goodbye to Lai while he was leaving the newsroom.

"You are still welcome to come back and write on a project-to-project basis," said Lai.

Without answering, Solomon closed the door to the newsroom and headed out of the China Courier building one last time.

The next day, Solomon boarded China Airlines CI006 to Los Angeles.

CHAPTER 16

Ma Ying-jeou's campaign for the 2008 presidential elections gained momentum with his acquittal from the corruption trial as the Kuomintang candidate began a fifteen-day bicycle tour of southern Taiwan along with his running mate, former premier Vincent Siew.

Ma's charm offensive to the southern Taiwan counties of Tainan and Kaohsiung included stops at a hospital in the southern city Kaohsiung where he offered encouragement to the ill and a fish farm where he learned in front of the camera how to catch fish with his bare hands.

During the course of his bicycle journey, Ma would stay at the residences of private citizens as the Kuomintang candidate battled for votes in the southern Taiwan counties that were traditionally DPP strongholds.

Ma's bicycle tour proved successful as polls showed the Kuomintang candidate gaining points after the end of his trip.

As for the DPP, president Chen Shui-bian's inability to show flexibility in working with the gridlocked Legislature and confrontational remarks against mainland China have resulted in a slide in his popularity.

The same month when Ma was acquitted of corruption charges, the DPP announced that former premier Frank

Hsieh will run for the 2008 presidential elections along with running mate and former premier Su Tseng-chang.

―――――

MARCH 22, 2008

Late evening before the Central Election Commission tallied the final votes, the three terrestrial TV stations projected the victory of the Kuomintang pair Ma Ying-jeou and Vincent Siew over DPP ticket Frank Hsieh and Su Tseng-chang in the presidential elections.

Ma and Siew won the presidential race by over eighteen percent of the votes over Hsieh and Su in the landslide victory. Voter turnout was 76.33 percent, slightly lower than the 80.28 percent turnout in the 2004 presidential elections.

The next day president-elect Ma held a press conference announcing that he will work towards implementing the "Three Links," or shipping, transportation, and postal links with mainland China and improve cross-strait relations.

The Taiwan stock market reacted to Ma's policy announcement with a 534 point jump as companies in the transportation sector enjoyed gains in anticipation of the opening of the "Three Links" with mainland China.

―――――

JUNE, 2008

After his inauguration in May, President Ma Ying-jeou immediately worked towards a resumption of semi-official talks with mainland China on allowing mainland tour groups to Taiwan.

Chiang Pin-kun of Taiwan's Straits Exchange Foundation led a delegation to Beijing to discuss bringing mainland tourists to Taiwan, a task which former president Chen had failed to achieve.

By the end of June, the first mainland tour group set foot on Taiwan to the welcome of Taiwan businesses which carry hopes that the tour groups can help strengthen Taiwan's economy.

———

DECEMBER 2008

Association for Relations across the Taiwan Strait's Chen Yun Lin arrived in Taipei for the second round of the semi-official talks between Taiwan and mainland China. At the end of the meeting held at Taipei's Grand Hotel, Chen and Chiang Pin-kun of the Straits Exchange Foundation signed an agreement to formally launch the opening of the "Three Links."

In 2007, Taiwan received the number one ranking in press freedom in Asia by Reporters Without Borders, con-firming the contributions of the country's media industry to fulfilling the Taiwan public's right to know. Ignorance by the public is no less dangerous in a democracy as an inept government.

———

AUGUST 8, 2008

The Beijing Olympics opened to a ceremony of epic proportions which told a story from China's past to a modern nation. With elaborate fireworks, a drum troupe comprised of soldiers from the People's Liberation Army, dances by women in traditional costume, and a center electronic "scroll" screen playing out Chinese ink painting, the opening ceremony was considered the best there was.

Beijing Olympic Organizing Committee (BOOC) spent 15 billion U.S. dollars organizing the Olympics, including the construction of the "Bird's Nest" stadium and the adjacent "Water Cube," the venues for track and field and swimming, respectively. The cost of the 2008 Beijing Olympics was the highest ever, yet BOOC was praised for its thousands-strong team of volunteers to help the Olympics run smoothly.

Western media, which had long anticipated the 2008 Olympics as a "coming out" party for the PRC, billed the Beijing Olympics as a success even though mainland residents attending the event far outnumbered foreigners.

DECEMBER 8, 2008

Two Chinese maritime surveillance ships sailed six kilometers off the coast of the disputed Diaoyutai islands that were controlled by Japan in the East China Sea. The two ships stopped near the waters of Diaoyutai under the watch of a Japan Coast Guard patrol boat in a standoff that lasted nine hours.

The Japanese government immediately protested against the mainland China government over the incident.

PRC's ministry of foreign affairs responded by claiming that China had the right to patrol the waters of the Diaoyutai Islands since the islands have always been a part of China's territory.

Two months later, the Japan Maritime Safety Agency deployed PLHs, or patrol vessels that can accommodate the take-off and landing of helicopters, in the waters near Diaoyutai in an attempt to defend against the "invasion" of Chinese maritime surveillance ships.

One month later, Japanese prime minister Taro Aso referred to Diaoyutai islands as a part of Japanese territory twice during his visit to the U.S. Aso added that the islands are protected by the Japan-U.S. security treaty.

DECEMBER 23, 2009

A U.S. defense contractor Raytheon received a contract approved by Taiwan's Legislature to manufacture 200 PAC-3 missiles for the R.O.C. The U.S.'s Department of Defense gave clearance for the contract in the face of opposition from the PRC.

Two months later, the PRC foreign ministry expressed anger at the U.S.'s arms sale to Taiwan which included Blackhawk helicopters and anti-missile systems added to the original package.

Vice foreign minister He Yafei told the government mouthpiece Xinhua News Agency that "China had strongly protested the U.S. government's recent decision to allow Raytheon and Lockheed Martin to sell weapons to Taiwan which would undermine national security."

———

The flower beds sit on the banks of the river as it runs
west
Towards the endless time the current carries to its rest
At the lake the water sits still waiting as the sun sets
All we can do is sit at the shore and breathe a sigh with
gest

I carry on with the secrets hidden in my chest
I know from now on I will be free from the times of pests
The fools and the ignorant may gather around one last
time to remember
That once it was just another time coming around in
December

May the enlightened do no more to me than is already
done
So that we may walk towards the bright orange sun
With that sense of hope that me miss so much and that
had been undone
That made us faltered at every step and pull the deadly
gun

May the winds blow hope like the ships centuries ago
Afore to the mark of purpose and love we go
Step by step together with the lasting song
From here to there and wherever the heart longs

———

———

FEBRUARY 5, 2009

Solomon and Aunt Victoria returned home from a three-day trip to Las Vegas only to learn that their home in Arcadia had been burglarized. All the jewelry which Aunt Victoria hid in a drawer was stolen, along with a small amount of cash as clothing and picture frames lay scattered across Solomon and Aunt Victoria's rooms. The total loss was minimal, but Solomon decided to call police anyway.

Two Arcadia police officers knocked on Solomon's door and pressed the doorbell fifteen minutes after the call.

Solomon answered the door.

"We received a call that your house was burglarized?" one of the officers said.

"Yes, please come in." said Solomon.

The two officers entered the house and began to check the house room by room.

Solomon showed the officers the drawer which contained the lost jewelry and a hundred dollars in cash.

"We found this when we returned from Las Vegas," said Solomon.

"Usually in this circumstance, it is difficult for us to apprehend the burglar," said one of the officers. "However, you can file a police report in case any leads will come up in the future."

"I want to file a police report," said Solomon.

The two officers began questioning Solomon on the time of day when he returned home, the length of time when he went away from home, a description of the items stolen from the house, and personal information.

After filling in the information in their notebooks, the two officers said goodbye and left Solomon and Aunt Victoria's house.

_____

APRIL. 9, 2009

Chief Lu Chen of the PRC Ministry of State Security's second bureau posted on the office bulletin board a notification for a meeting of all his staff members. After the entire staff was present at the conference room, Lu walked in and started the meeting.

"Comrades, I have received an order from the minister to launch a surveillance operation in Los Angeles," said Lu.

The second bureau was the MSS's arm for foreign intelligence gathering.

"Our subject is an American citizen of Chinese descent," said Lu. "He has worked as a journalist in Taiwan at an English newspaper, The China Courier."

"According to our sources, the subject now resides in Los Angeles," said Lu while giving each of his staff a file containing Solomon's basic information.

"Our intelligence has revealed that Solomon Woo has been living in Arcadia, Los Angeles for the past two years," said Lu.

"Our mission, code-named Operation Dragon Eye, is to place Solomon under surveillance and find out what he knows about us," said Lu. "The minister has given us the order to eliminate Solomon if it is discovered that he is working for the U.S. or Taiwan intelligence agencies."

"I have chosen Hong Kai, Chi Yun, and Shen Dong to execute the mission in L.A. due to your weapons experience in the People's Liberation Army," said Lu.

"Our local contact in Los Angeles is a realtor named Wendy Shi whom Hong, Chi, and Shen will meet in L.A." said Lu.

MAY 12, 2009

Shen Dong walked through the front door of Sina-Mex shipping agency in the Mexican port city of Puerto de Manzanillo after a three hour drive from Mexico City. The mainland China operative had just flew into Mexico City in the morning with a Brunei passport and tourist visa.

Despite the jet lag, Shen rented a Chevy Malibu at the airport using a Union Pay debit card issued in China and on the same day drove to Manzanillo due west of Mexico City.

No one was behind the counter at Sina-Mex shipping agency when Shen entered. Shen noticed a doorway at the back of the room leading to what seemed like a warehouse.

"Is anybody there?" Shen yelled out towards the doorway.

Immediately, a clerk of Asian descent emerged from the warehouse dressed in a red T-shirt and blue jeans.

"How can I help you?" the clerk said.

"I am here to pick up a package," said Shen.

"I need to see your I.D. and a copy of the invoice,"

Shen reached into his backpack and took out his Brunei passport along with the invoice of the package that was shipped from mainland China. The mainland operative calmly handed the two documents to the clerk.

"Hold on," the clerk said before disappearing into the warehouse.

Ten minutes later, the Asian clerk returned to the counter carrying a sealed cardboard box.

"Please sign here," the clerk said as he produced a notebook.

Shen signed on the notebook which contained all of the agency's shipments.

"Here is your package," said the clerk.

Shen carried the box out of the agency and into his car. The former People's Liberation Army colonel checked that no one was around and then opened the package which contained three 9 millimeter Berettas and five army-issued hand grenades. Shen placed the contents of the package into his backpack and drove off towards to Hotel Manzanita late in the evening.

After checking in at the hotel, Shen laid down all his luggage and the backpack containing the weapons in his room. He then took the elevator down to the lobby and placed a phone call to MSS from a public phone.

The MSS operator answered the call.

"Name and bureau, please," the operator said.

"Shen Dong, second bureau," Shen said.

"Hold on," said the operator as she connected..

Lu answered the phone.

"This is Lu Chen,"

"This is Shen Dong. I received the package." Shen said.

"Good," Lu said before hanging up.

After a good night's sleep, Shen woke up and began to pack his belongings for the long drive to Los Angeles. The former colonel removed the spare tire from the trunk and hid the backpack in the empty compartment, closing the cover shut.

Shen drove the Malibu with Mexican license plates for ten hours before reaching the U.S.-Mexico border at Tijuana. A two-mile stretch of stop and go traffic at the U.S. border checkpoint delayed Shen as he joined in the wait. Two hours later in the early evening, Shen came to the border checkpoint while a Customs and Border Protection officer flagged him down. Shen presented his Brunei passport and international driver's license to the officer.

"What is your purpose of visiting the U.S.?" the officer asked.

"I am here for sightseeing," said Shen. "I also have relatives in Los Angeles whom I want to visit?" said Shen.

"Where in Los Angeles do your relatives live?" the officer asked.

"In Pasadena," said Shen.

The officer looked through Shen's passport and found the U.S. tourist visa.

"Where else in the U.S. will you visit," the officer pressed on.

"I will visit Arizona and Utah," Shen said.

The officer nodded and gave the documents back to Shen, signaling for him to pass.

———

Two hours later, Shen arrived at Wendy Shi's residence in Pasadena which became a temporary safe house for Operation Dragon Eye. Shen knocked on the door of Shi's house. A few moments later, Shi opened the door.

"I am Shen Dong," said Shen.

"Come in," said Shi.

"Are Hong Kai and Chi Yun here?" asked Shen.

"They will fly in tomorrow," said Shi.

The next day, Shen Dong left Shi's residence at 10 a.m. and drove to the Tom Bradley International Airport to pick up Hong Kai and Chi Yun. Hong and Chi disembarked from their Air China flight from Beijing at 10:05 a.m. and joined the long queue at immigration and customs. The mainland operatives were allowed to pass immigration on Brunei passports.

Half an hour later, Hong and Chi picked up their luggage and walked out to the arrivals hall where they were met by Shen.

Without a word, Shen led the way to the airport parking lotand helped Hong and Chi load their luggage onto the Malibu.

"Did you have any trouble at the Mexican border?" Hong asked Shen.

"No" said Shen before driving off from the airport.

Fifty minutes later, the Operation Dragon Eye team came to a stop along the curb outside of Shi's three bedroom house. Shi just finished cooking when Shen, Hong, and Chi were standing outside her front door. She opened the door and let the team in.

"I just finished cooking," said Shi. "Come to the dining room after you lay your luggage down."

The team gathered at the dining table to a simple meal consisted of Kung Pao Chicken, broccoli beef, and fried eggs.

Shi's house in Pasadena was only five miles away from Solomon's residence in the affluent neighborhood of Arcadia. As a realtor, Shi had been given the task to find a house near Solomon's home that would serve as a base for the surveillance operation.

Two weeks ago, Shi located a house three doors down from Solomon's house which was available for sale. With funds wired from a private account belonging to MSS bureau chief Lu Chen, Shi purchased the house at a cost of US$900,000.

Shi placed a call to MSS the day the sale was made.

"I have purchased the house that we wanted near

Solomon's home," said Shi. "As soon as we obtain our laser surveillance equipment, we can move in."

"Okay," said Lu Chen.

The next day, Shi called her friend Mary Cai, a mainland China and U.S. dual citizen who owns Hollywood Stunts, a company providing stuntmen to movie studios in Hollywood. Cai had been asked by Shi to purchase laser surveillance equipment under the company's name.

"Hi, Mary." said Shi.

"Hello," said Cai.

"Do you have the surveillance equipment yet?" said Shi.

"Yes, I just purchased the laser surveillance equipment that you wanted today from a security company in Venice," said Cai. "The equipment comes in four metal cases and is still in our truck. Where do you want me to move it?"

"503 Arbolada Drive in Arcadia," said Shi. "Can you bring the equipment over today?"

"Yes."

Cai summoned one of her employees to drive the company truck which bear the sign "Hollywood Stunts" from their Hollywood office to Arcadia with Cai riding on the passenger side.

By late afternoon, Cai and her driver backed up the truck onto the driveway of the Arcadia house with Shi, Shen, Hong, and Chi waiting outside. The four MSS operatives unloaded the four metal cases and carried them into the house.

Shi wrote out a personal check for $38,000 and gave it to Cai for the cost of the surveillance equipment before saying goodbye.

The set of laser surveillance equipment included a laser transmitter, a laser receiver, and an amplifier with audio recorder. Without entering the subject's house, the laser equipment functions by picking up audio within the house through vibrations on the window pane which are then reflected to the laser receiver up to 500 meters away.

CHAPTER 17

MAY 14, 2009

Solomon peeked out the window of his bedroom at approximately 4:15 p.m. and spotted a white truck with the sign Hollywood Stunts drive past his home and pull up to a driveway of a house three doors down on Arbolada Drive.

That evening, Solomon was watching a Taiwan talk show program through a satellite television provider when he heard a loud chirp of a bird that was then drowned out by a high-pitched whistle just outside his living room window.

Solomon had anticipated this day since a few months ago when Taiwan's arms procurement proposal was approved by the Taiwan Legislature and the U.S. Department of Defense amid an escalating territorial dispute between the PRC and U.S. ally Japan over the Diaoyutai Islands.

MAY 15, 2009

As Solomon stepped into his Toyota Camry on his driveway, he noticed a Volvo parked along the curb in front of the house three doors down. From about one hundred meters away, Solomon saw a middle-aged Asian man in a jacket sitting in the driver's seat.

Solomon drove off towards the Arcadia Mall two miles away as part of his daily routine to read at the bookstore.

The former journalist saw the Volvo behind him as he was waiting to make the turn on to Baldwin Avenue where the mall was located. The Volvo remained at Solomon's tail as he turned into the mall parking lot. Solomon parked his car into a spot near the mall entrance when the Volvo drove past behind him and parked in the next row.

Solomon stepped off his Camry and entered the mall, walking calmly towards his destination. The thirty-five year old Solomon kept his stride and came to the bookstore where he picked up an Economist magazine from the magazine stands.

Ten minutes later, Solomon spotted the Asian man in the Volvo browsing the stands inside the bookstore.

Solomon finished reading the Economist magazine and left the bookstore one hour later.

Maintaining a deliberate pace, Solomon came to the McDonald's inside the mall and ordered an ice cream cone. With no sign of the man in the Volvo, Solomon left the mall and returned home.

That night after dinner, Solomon set out on a walk around his neighborhood for his daily exercise. Halfway through his walk around the block, the man in a jacket whom Solomon recognized earlier driving the Volvo walked towards him from a distance. Just as the two approached each other, the man turned his back against Solomon and showed a 9 millimeter Beretta tucked into his belt.

A frightened Solomon continued on his way around the block and returned home.

The following night, Solomon met the same man on his

evening walk as the two passed each other again this time without incident. The same routine would continue every day for the next month.

———

JUNE 16, 2009

CIA deputy director Adams was watching the day's satellite surveillance video feed on Solomon's house and the former journalist's daily encounters with the mainland China operative when he decided to take action to end the mainland China threat.

Adams walked into the office of CIA director George Flannigan holding a DVD recorded off the day's satellite surveillance feed over Solomon's house and the neighboring house that was being occupied by the mainland China operatives in Arcadia.

"Here is today's satellite video of Solomon's house," said Adams, while handing over the disc to Flannigan.

"It is time to end the threat," said Adams. "We should let the FBI handle this."

After a long pause, Flannigan turned to his computer and sent a memorandum to the FBI via e-mail:

To: FBI director Tom Grey

From: CIA director George Flannigan.

Subject: PRC espionage activity

Director Grey,

We have discovered a team of Chinese covert operatives engaging in espionage activity in Los

Angeles. Three mainland China nationals armed with 9 millimeter Berettas and hand grenades have been conducting surveillance on an American citizen in Arcadia, Los Angeles County starting one month ago.

The American citizen worked as a reporter in Taiwan and has been residing in Arcadia, California for the last two years.

The PRC operatives have equipped themselves with laser surveillance technology at a house one hundred meters away from the American's residence. The operatives pose a threat to the neighborhood in Arcadia.

I advise the FBI to take action to remove the threat before the situation escalates.

Satellite surveillance videos of the PRC operatives' activity will be given to you by one of my staff tomorrow morning.

———

JUNE 17, 2009

Los Angeles County District Attorney Jackie Mitchell received a phone call from FBI director Tom Grey in the morning.

"This is Mitchell," said the district attorney.

"Hi, this is FBI director Tom Grey. I have a case here that falls under your jurisdiction,"

"What is it?"

"A team of Chinese covert operatives has been conducting illegal surveillance on an American citizen living in

Arcadia," said Grey. "The operatives are armed with 9 millimeter Berettas and hand grenades and pose a threat to the neighborhood."

"Who is the American citizen," Mitchell asked.

"His name is Solomon Woo. He worked as a journalist in Taiwan," said Grey. "The CIA alerted me to this matter yesterday."

"The Chinese operatives have stationed themselves in a house one hundred meters away from Solomon's residence in Arcadia," said Grey.

"A package containing satellite surveillance videos of the PRC operatives' activity was sent today and should arrive at your office tomorrow morning along with information on the American," said Grey.

———

JUNE 19, 2009

A search warrant was issued by Los Angeles Superior Court judge Thomas Roberts on the PRC operatives' house in Arcadia based on the satellite surveillance video provided by district attorney Mitchell.

The Los Angeles Police Department SWAT team was given the order to carry out the raid on the PRC house at midnight when Hong, Chi, and Shen were sleeping. LAPD also mobilized a helicopter to support the SWAT operation.

Armed with semi-automatic rifles and wearing night vision goggles, a team of seven SWAT team members descended on 503 Arbolada Drive in Arcadia in a van, stopping just short of the driveway five minutes before midnight.

The SWAT team stepped off the truck and quickly took

their positions outside the front door of the house in two files, as one team member prepared to break into the residence with a battering ram.

With two strikes, the SWAT team broke open the front door and entered the house.

Sleeping in one bedroom, Shen and Chi were immediately awakened by the sound of the break-in. Just as the two ran out to retrieve their guns in the living room, the operatives were met by two SWAT team members.

"Stop.! Raise your hands. This is LAPD," said one of the two SWAT members with their rifles pointed at the PRC operatives.

Shen and Chi stopped and raised their arms.

"Lay down on the ground," said the SWAT member.

Shen and Chi lied down as the two SWAT members handcuffed them.

The remaining five SWAT members continued on their sweep of the house searching for the third operative, Hong Kai, when they heard glass breaking from the master bedroom. Three SWAT members, including team leader Victor Olson hurried to the master bedroom only to find the window broken.

Olson radioed in to LAPD dispatch.

"Dispatch, this is SWAT team 3. Two suspects have been apprehended with one on the loose. Request assistance from Arcadia PD and local county sheriff." Olson said over the roar of the LAPD helicopter hovering over the house. "Chopper 3, I need an aerial search for the suspect on Hesperia Street."

Two SWAT members loaded Shen and Chi into the SWAT truck as team leader Olson split the remaining members into two teams with one following Hong over the backyard fence and the other, including himself, pursuing the operative from Arbolada Drive.

Well trained in the military, Hong ran for half a mile from Hesperia Street and onto Baldwin Avenue without breaking stride. Just as he approached the Los Angeles Arboretum, Hong was spotted by the LAPD helicopter which captured him with its search light. The helicopter pilot radioed to Olson.

"SWAT team 3, this is Chopper 3.

"I have the suspect running on foot along Baldwin Avenue," said the helicopter pilot.

"Copy," said Olson as he looked up at the helicopter search light aiming south from his position.

Realizing that he was spotted by the helicopter, Hong ran towards the entrance of the Los Angeles Arboretum and climbed the front gate into the arboretum grounds.

"SWAT team 3, I just lost the suspect," said the helicopter pilot. "He has just climbed the gate into the Los Angeles Arboretum."

Ten minutes later, all seven of the SWAT team members gathered outside the front gate of the arboretum, joined by Arcadia Police Department officers and Los Angeles County Sheriff, including a K-9 unit.

Half an hour later, a perimeter was set up that sealed the area of the arboretum from Baldwin Avenue in the east to Colorado Blvd. to the north.

Before long, a total of twenty police officers were combing through the arboretum looking for the suspect.

Hong finally stopped running after finding the Queen Anne Cottage, a historic two story house built in the late nineteenth century on the south side of the arboretum. Hong turned the door knob of the house's front door and discovered it was unlocked. Climbing to the second floor of the house, Hong hid himself inside a bedroom with a window facing a lake.

In the darkness, the K-9 unit of the Los Angeles County Sheriff led the way for the police's search for Hong. As the K-9 unit came upon Queen Anne Cottage, the dog barked loudly at the house and at the county sheriff officer, who radioed in for backup.

Ten minutes later, the SWAT team assembled outside the Queen Anne Cottage taking positions at all four corners around the house. Olson sounded his warning to Hong.

"This is LAPD. You are surrounded. Come out with your hands up," said Olson.

Five minutes passed without a response from Hong.

Olson radioed to his SWAT members to prepare for an assault through the front door. The team leader decided to keep the four corner perimeter around the house and take two SWAT members with him inside.

Moving in behind the point man, Olson entered the house and began to take the stairs to the second floor in the darkness when his assault team was fired upon from upstairs. Olson and his team fired back.

The first exchange of gun fire resulted in an injury to the lower leg of Olson's point man as he fell to the floor.

Olson reached for the stun grenade on his belt and pulled the pin before tossing it upstairs to the second floor. The huge explosion shook the house with pieces of wood falling from the ceiling.

The SWAT team leader and his team member behind him charged up the stairs to the second floor and heard the sound of Hong running for cover inside one of the bedrooms. From the second floor, Olson radioed quietly to his team members outside.

"This is Olson. If you have a clear shot, take the man out," said Olson.

Olson and his assault team member quietly moved into

one of two bedrooms on the second floor. Wearing night vision goggles, Olson found no sign of Hong in the first bedroom. As he prepared to sweep through the second bedroom, Olson heard the sound of a window opening coming from the inside.

Olson radioed quietly to his team members.

"Suspect is inside the bedroom facing west," said Olson.

One of the SWAT team members outside spotted Hong trying to open the window on the west side of the house.

"I see him," said the SWAT team member, who was securing the northwest perimeter outside of the house.

With laser sighting on his scope, the SWAT team member aimed at Hong's head with his semi-automatic rifle and took the shot. The bullet hit Hong in the forehead, killing the PRC operative instantly.

CHAPTER 18

Secretary of State Roger Fulman was awakened by a phone call at his residence at 4:30 in the morning by Under Secretary for Political Affairs Patrick Edelman.

"Who is this," said Fulman.

"This is Under Secretary Edelman. There is an emergency situation. Two Chinese nationals armed with guns and grenades have been arrested early this morning in Los Angeles for committing espionage activity on an American citizen.

One other PRC national was shot and killed by LAPD SWAT team after firing at the SWAT officers.

Laser surveillance equipment was found at the house of the PRC operatives located less than 100 meters away from the American's residence," said Edelman.

"Who is this American?" asked Fulman.

"He was a journalist at a newspaper in Taiwan," said Edelman.

"LAPD and the Los Angeles District Attorney are waiting on whether they should press charges on the two PRC nationals," said Edelman.

"Tell them to hold on," said Fulman. "Call a meeting with assistant secretary Vincent Kao and the staff of the East Asian and Pacific Affairs bureau now at the bureau's conference room. Also, tell LAPD and the District Attorney to keep the press out of this."

At six in the morning, the entire staff of the East Asian and Pacific Affairs bureau, assistant secretary Kao, and Under Secretary Edelman were present at the conference room before Fulman entered to start the meeting.

"Who has a report for me?" asked Fulman.

Under Secretary Edelman stood up and handed a file to Fulman containing details of the PRC espionage case.

"How did these PRC nationals enter U.S?" asked Fulman.

"All three of them carried Brunei passports and entered on tourist visas," said Edelman.

"We can charge them with illegal surveillance on U.S. soil or possession of illegal weapons," Edelman said.

"Both would have to be tried at federal court," said Fulman. "I don't want this matter to drag on forever. Before I call the PRC Foreign Minister, I want to know everything about this American."

A long silence fell upon the conference room before assistant secretary Kao spoke.

"The American citizen's name is Solomon," said Assistant Secretary Kao. Born in the United States, the Chinese American attended university here and went on to work for an English newspaper in Taiwan for three years. We are in the process of gathering all of his clips."

"O.K." said Fulman.

"Does anyone have the list of dissidents under house arrest in PRC on hand?" asked Fulman. A staff member took out a State Department report containing a list of detained PRC dissidents and gave it to Fulman. The Secretary of State looked through the list when one familiar name, Gao Zhisheng, caught his eye. The human rights attorney in China had a record of defending activists and religious minorities and has written a book "A China More Just" in 2007, Fulman recalled. Gao had been subsequently detained and tortured in 2007 by PRC secret police. The PRC foreign ministry said that Gao was imprisoned on charges of subversion of state power and disturbing public order.

———

Fulman returned to his office and placed a call to PRC Foreign Minister Chuang Wei Min.

"Foreign minister's office," a female receptionist answered.

"I need to speak with Minister Chuang,"

"Please hold," the receptionist said while connecting the call.

"This is Chuang,"

"Hi, Minister Chuang. This is Secretary Fulman. There is a situation here in the U.S. which should concern you. The Los Angeles Police Department has arrested two PRC nationals for engaging in espionage activity. A third PRC national was killed by LAPD after firing at the officers."

LAPD has confiscated laser surveillance equipment, three hand guns, and hand grenades inside a house in Los Angeles where the three stayed. The two PRC nationals detained by police are Chi Yun, and Shen Dong. The PRC national killed was Hong Kai.

"Are you aware of the espionage activity?" asked Fulman.

"No, I am not." said Chuang.

"I have instructed LAPD and the LA county district attorney to hold off filing charges against the two PRC citizens," said Fulman.

"Please give me some time while I look into this matter," said Chuang. "I will call you back."

———

"Sure," said Fulman.

———

Right after the phone call with Secretary Fulman, Minister Chuang placed a call to Minister of State Security Wong Chi Cong.

"Hi, This is minister Chuang Wei Min,"

"Hello, What can I do for you?" said Wong.

"I just received a phone call from U.S. Secretary Fulman who said that the Los Angeles Police Department has arrested two PRC citizens for espionage while killing another. The two detained are Chi Yun and Shen Dong, and the one killed was Hong Kai.

"Are you aware of this?" asked Chuang.

After a long pause, Wong decided to divulge his knowledge of Operation Dragon Eye.

"It is our MSS operation in Los Angeles," said Wong. "Can you ask the U.S. Secretary of State to release our operatives?"

"I'll try," said Chuang and hung up.

Half an hour after Fulman spoke to Chuang, the foreign minister telephoned back on a direct line to the Secretary of State's office.

"Fulman speaking,"

"Hello, Secretary Fulman. This is Chuang,"

"I have spoken to our Minister of State Security who confirmed there was such an espionage operation," said Chuang. "We request that you release the detained agents and return them to China, along with the body of the slain operative."

"The United States can return your agents to China upon

one condition: that you release Gao Zhisheng from prison," said Fulman.

"I can't make a decision on that in my position," said Chuang. "I will have to relay your message to the Politburo."

———

It was noon when the nine-member Politburo standing committee and Minister of State Security Wong Chi Cong gathered for an emergency meeting inside the Zhongnanhai compound in Beijing. PRC President Hu Jintao started the meeting.

"Comrades, Foreign Minister Chuang Wei Min has informed me that one of our covert operations in the United States has been compromised. Two of our agents have been arrested by Los Angeles Police Department while one other was killed.

Minister Chuang has requested that the U.S. release our agents and return them to China.

The U.S. side, however, demanded that we release Gao Zhisheng in exchange for the repatriation of the two agents.

"Gao was the lawyer who wrote the book `A China More Just', right?" asked committee member Li Keqiang.

"Yes," said Hu. "Our Public Security Bureau has put him under house arrest at his home in Taiyuan, Shanxi Province."

"Gao could start more trouble if we release him," said committee member Wang Qishan.

"We have to take that risk before the cases escalates into an international incident." said Hu. "Tell the Public Security Bureau to release Gao."

Consular officer Samuel Tate waited outside the gate of the U.S. embassy in Beijing for the Beijing Public Security Bureau. Tate was ordered by Ambassador Bowman to travel to Taiyuan, Shanxi province with the PSB and act as a witness to the release of dissident Gao Zhisheng.

At 10:00 a.m. sharp, two Beijing PSB patrol cars pulled up before the gate of the U.S. embassy. A PSB officer stepped out of the rear car and approached Tate.

"Are you Samuel Tate?" the officer asked.

"Yes," said Tate.

"Please come with me."

Tate and the officer stepped into the back of the patrol car. Trailing the front car, Tate and the Beijing PSB officers drove to the fifth ring road on the outskirts of Beijing before merging onto the expressway towards Taiyuan.

Seven hours later, the Beijing PSB officer in the front car called Taiyuan PSB station with his cell phone as they entered Taiyuan city limits.

"This is Beijing PSB. We shall arrive in twenty minutes," the officer said.

"Good, we will wait for you outside," said a Taiyuan PSB officer.

Twenty minutes later, Tate and the Beijing PSB pulled up in front of the Taiyuan PSB station where one Taiyuan patrol car was waiting. A Taiyuan officer stepped out of the car and came to the Beijing PSB patrol cars.

"I will lead you to Gao's residence," said the Taiyuan PSB officer.

The three cars drove for ten minutes and came to a

one-story house surrounded by a wall on all four sides, a traditional Chinese courtyard residence, with two Taiyuan PSB officers guarding the front gate. One of the Beijing PSB officers showed a Politburo document signed by Hu that authorized the end of Gao's arrest to the guards.

The two guards read the document and signaled Tate and the other PSB officers to follow them in.

Gao was reading a book "The Details of Democracy," in his bedroom when Tate and the group of PSB officers appeared.

"Gao Zhisheng, You are now free," the PSB guard said while handing him the Politburo document.

By 6 p.m., Tate and all of the PSB officers left Gao's residence as the Beijing PSB drove towards a hotel to stay the night. Arriving at the hotel, Tate called the Ambassador Bowman at the U.S. embassy in Beijing with his cell phone.

"This is Bowman,"

"Mr. Ambassador, This is Tate. The PSB ended Gao's house arrest."

"Good," said Bowman.

_____

THE NEXT DAY,

At 10:00 a.m., Secretary Fulman received the word of Gao's release and immediately placed a telephone call to Immigration and Customs Enforcement (ICE) director Bill Elliot.

"Hello, this is Eliot,"

"Director Eliot, this is Secretary Fulman,"

"Did you read the report on the PRC spies I sent you?"

"Yes, I have,"

"The two PRC spies have entered the United States on forged passports. They should be immediately repatriated to China."

"Yes, Mr. Secretary. I will inform our officers to take custody of the PRC spies."

————

Shi and Shen were escorted by a team of ICE agents to the Tom Bradley International Airport after spending days in the LAPD detention center. The agents uncuffed the two PRC nationals before watching them enter the departure gate and board an Air China flight bound for Beijing.

On the same day, the body of Hong Kai was returned to Beijing via an Air China cargo flight.

————

JANUARY 9, 2010

It was the first time that Solomon returned to Hong Kong after his father died there eight years ago. The Cathay Pacific flight from Los Angeles to Hong Kong brought Solomon to the Chek Lap Kok Airport, Hong Kong's glitzy, new airport built at the time of Hong Kong's handover to the PRC.

Clearing customs, Solomon took the Airport Express train to Central subway station on Hong Kong island and checked in at the Central Park Hotel at 3 p.m.

After laying his luggage down in his room, Solomon headed towards the minibus station in Central and boarded the minibus which took him to the Hong Kong Chinese Christian Cemetery.

The rows of graves in the cemetery were arranged by alphabetical order. Solomon found his father's grave and took a moment before he bowed.

CPSIA information can be obtained
at www.ICGtesting.com
Printed in the USA
BVHW041559240719
554236BV00016B/695/P